Socrates without Tears

The Lost Dialogues of Aeschines Restored

Socrates without Tears

The Lost Dialogues of Aeschines Restored

Alan Jacobs

BOOKS

Winchester, UK
Washington, USA

First published by O-Books, 2011
O-Books is an imprint of John Hunt Publishing Ltd., Laurel House, Station Approach,
Alresford, Hants, SO24 9JH, UK
office1@o-books.net
www.o-books.com

For distributor details and how to order please visit the 'Ordering' section on our website.

Text copyright: Alan Jacobs 2011

ISBN: 978 1 84694 568 7

A CIP catalogue record for this book is available from the British Library.

Design: Lee Nash

Printed in the UK by CPI Antony Rowe
Printed in the USA by Offset Paperback Mfrs, Inc

We operate a distinctive and ethical publishing philosophy in all
areas of our business, from our global network of authors to
production and worldwide distribution.

CONTENTS

Prelude

Socrates

Sage of Wisdom! all who hear you must admit,
Your words carry the wind-swift speed of civic wit.
You've mastered every weather in your speech,
Fierce nipping words that coldly freeze yet teach.
You shower sharp arrow-barbs, sent to defy
Opponents beneath the stormy winter sky.
Before you, all contenders are bound to fall,
While your bright Sun of Wisdom shines light on all.

After Thucydides

Chapter 1

The Momentous Discovery of Dr. Ernest R. Sekers

My most revered colleague and life long friend, the late Dr. Ernest R. Sekers (1949-2009), gave me written permission, before his recent, sudden and tragic death, well before his time, to write a full account of his greatest discovery, and publish, albeit posthumously his valuable findings.

Dr. Ernest R. Sekers, as we all know, was universally acknowledged as the leading and most respected Classical Greek Scholar of his generation. He was overjoyed to have discovered some of the missing Socratic Dialogues and Memorabilia recorded by Aeschines Socraticus (c.400 BC) which had been missing for over fifteen hundred years and were presumed to have been lost since ancient times.

While on a well earned Academic Sabbatical in Cairo, where it was his custom to take frequent exploratory voyages up and down the River Nile, in search of Classical Greek Inscriptions, a momentous event happened. These ancient inscriptions were generally left on artefacts, and were inscribed during the Greek occupation, at the time of the decaying Egyptian Civilisation.

On his last but fateful visit, Ernest was solicited by an itinerant Bedouin labourer. The man had recently been employed on one of the many archaeological excavations sponsored by the Egyptian Ministry of Culture and Antiquities. As Ernest related this momentous event to me, the man, whom he vaguely recognised from previous visits, had approached him with words which amounted to "Esteemed and worthy Sir, I have been waiting for you, and I knew you would one day come, I have found some very ancient Greek papyri for you, they are most important, please, I beg of you, do take your time and have a good look!" Dr.Sekers was mildly intrigued; he always followed up these unsolicited approaches, but never expected to find anything of much importance. He had been offered many manuscripts before which invariably turned out to be the household accounts of some nobleman, civil servant or minor military official. Anyhow, Dr.Sekers conscientiously and carefully opened the packet well wrapped up and tied. He saw tattered sheaves of papyri with somewhat faded and eroded Greek inscriptions written on them in an educated hand. Scanning them quickly, he caught sight of the word Socrates and asked the Arab where he had found them. The Bedouin said that that they had been deeply buried in a small amphora and tightly sealed. They had come to light when he and other workers were excavating near the site of what had once been the Great Library of Alexandria. This caught Dr. Sekers's interest and after some hard bargaining decided to buy the packet for what he considered to be a very small sum, that same afternoon.

Returning to his hotel room in Cairo, he carefully perused the contents and was convinced that these papyri definitely contained a number of Socratic Dialogues. He could tell that stylistically they were written neither by Plato, Xenophon nor Aristophanes. Then he realised with a sudden shock that he must be holding none other than some of the missing dialogues of no less a figure than Aeschines Socraticus. I remember years ago, Earnest telling me what a tragedy it was that the Aeschines Socraticus' Dialogues had all been lost, presumably forever. It seemed, intuitively he had felt that they would reveal a very different picture than those of the widely accepted and obviously sanitised Platonic records. It was if Plato was always trying to establish his own ambition to forge a reputation as a Philosopher for the benefit of his planned Academy, rather than faithfully transmit the spirit and content of Socrates' Dialogues precisely. Aeschines, was known to lean the other way and was reputed by contemporaries to be more trenchant and honest, if sometimes ribald in his handling of exchanges, as well as wryly humorous. Perhaps somewhat closer to Xenophon's rather more robust characterisation of the Master. Aeschines was known to colourfully display Socrates irony and sardonic wit. which Plato, with his mock seriousness, tended to underplay.

From my own researches, most of what we know about Aeschines (425-350 BC) better known as Aeschines Socraticus of Sphettus, comes from the reliable Diogenes Laertes in his book 'The Lives of Eminent Philosophers'. Aeschines is not to be confused with the famous Attic orator, of the same name (389-314 BC), the son of Atrometus. In Chapter VII Diogenes tells us that Aeschines Socraticus, was the son of Charinus, the Sausage Maker; but according to some other accounts he was the son of Lysanius. He was however, definitely a pupil of Socrates. There is also a recorded trial proceeding concerning Aeschines which tells us that at one time he fell into financial difficulties and incurred a debt while working as a perfume vendor and was unable to pay it back.

The famed Dr. Benjamin Jowett, the translator of all Plato's Dialogues, wrote about Aeschines Socraticus. "From the account of Diogenes Laertes, he appears to have been a familiar friend of his great master who said that 'of the sausage-seller's son, only he knew how to honour him.' The same writer has preserved the trusted tradition that it was actually Aeschines, and not Crito, who offered to assist Socrates in an escape from imprisonment."

Aeschines seems to have spent the greater part of his life in what we could call 'small poverty', which gave rise to Socrates advising him 'to borrow money from himself, instead of from others, by diminishing his daily wants.' He assisted his father in Sausage Manufacture before his own business failure as A Perfume Vendor. He then retired to the Syracusan Court where his friendship with Aristipus was reciprocated because of their common dislike of Plato. He stayed there until the expulsion of

3

one of his friends, the younger Dionysius, and returned to Athens where he gave private lectures on Philosophy. Plato falsely accused him of being a Sophist because he received money for this instruction. The three scant Dialogues which have survived are not considered genuine by contemporary scholars, as they do not contain the fullness of Socratic irony nor are they are elegant in style. Dr.Seker's important discovery, however, reveals some further Dialogues and Memorablia which are very different in character, and contain many new insights about Socrates which were, for some obscure reason, concealed by Plato and Xenophon. The recorders of all the Dialogues worked mainly from memory with some notes. Accounts therefore, vary considerably, and each reporter imposed his own gloss on what Socrates and others actually said. Although the events here are approximately the same as Xenophon's and in the case of Ion, Plato's account, they are more risqué, and also seem to show a clear link with the Non-Dual Brahmin Philosophers who the Roman Historian Josephus records as having visited Athens at that time. Many scholars have suggested that Socrates must have known some of the content of the Upanishads. There was considerable cultural and commercial interchange between Greece and India in this period, as my learned and esteemed colleague, Professor Dr. Hans Weisacre of Leipzig, to whom I have shown the translations of the original texts bequeathed to my by Dr.Sekers, has confirmed. He informed me that the Dialogues of Plato are not strictly reliable and quotes Diogenes Laertes as informing us that Socrates said "By Heracles! What a number of lies this young man [Plato] is telling about me!"

It was several months after his discovery, that with some trepidation, Ernest confided his great find to me, and handed me copies of his tentative translations for my candid opinion. "If anything ever happens to me, old boy, please see that they are published posthumously." That tragically was the last time I ever saw dear Ernest. Returning to Cairo for another trip he was found dead. He had been murdered, in one of Cairo's numerous back street alleys. He had been knifed and his wallet stolen along with his gold signet ring and wrist watch. Most readers will have read the many fulsome obituaries in the quality Daily Newspapers and Academic Press which appeared. I can only state that the translations he gave me were very far from being completed, and I had to considerably revise the draft in order to bring them forward for a suitable reading. They are certainly illuminating and I believe they have a great relevance to many of the contemporary questions posed by modern philosophy. They also vividly convey much of what we would call to-day 'the camp atmosphere' of the Socratic circle. In my view, it can truly be said that Aeschines Socraticus give us Plato without tears.

Chapter 2

Socrates Meets Aeschines
the Sausage Maker

Socrates: Hail to Thee, dear Aeschines, prince of sausage makers! Where are you coming from, to meet us now?

Aeschines: I have just come back from my father's kitchen. He is with me here [Socrates and Charinus acknowledge each other and exchange smiles], where I was assisting him in preparing his famed spiced meat delicacies.

Socrates: Yes! Charinus , your dear father, makes the finest sausages in all Athens, that is beyond any dispute.

Aeschines: Thank you, Socrates. Next to my own beloved father, I love you dearly. I hope I shall never, ever have to leave you. Even if you strike me with your staff, you will find no wood hard enough to keep me away from you, so long as I think you've something important to say. [This complement has also been quoted by Diogenes Laertes.]

Socrates: See! Only this sausage-maker's son knows how to honour me. I wish all my friends were as loyal as you, Aeschines. In some ways, your respected profession has often appealed to me as being most enviable. You assist your Father whom you love and cherish, you earn an honest livelihood, you exercise great care and attention. so keeping your restless monkey mind in check, and what is more, create marvellous delicacies for all the citizens of Athens to enjoy with their wine, and fill their bellies, which when digested, inspire good thoughts and hopefully beneficial actions.

Aeschines: You speak the truth as always, Socrates. I have toiled to excel at this work, selecting the choicest herbs and learning to pound the cooked rare meats into a fine paste and skilfully blend them, we pack them in an edible skin and make them look as appetising as possible.

Socrates: I am persuaded as to your eminent skill, Aeschines. I trust you will not refuse me a sample of your labours.

Aeschines: [opening his satchel] Here is one of Father's latest delicious concoctions, a mixture of equal parts of baby lamb and wild rabbit, flavoured with honey, thyme and black pepper.

Socrates: Thank you. I shall relish it more after our conversation but now ask me whatever question you will.

Aeschines: You said earlier that my food after being digested, stimulates or rather inspires thought which hopefully leads to action.

Socrates: I recall having said precisely that.

Aeschines: Does this mean I am indirectly responsible for my customer's thoughts and deeds?

Socrates: Listen both of you. After a fashion, partially, but not completely. Mind, obviously needs sufficient food stuff to make thoughts happen.

Aeschines: But surely Socrates, the man himself, is responsible for his own thoughts and actions, and has the freedom to decide his acts?

Socrates: Dear boy, I hope you will not be shocked when I tell you that man has no freedom of will, and is not really responsible for his actions. Nevertheless he must make every effort, from his false sense of himself which he calls 'me' to behave according to the highest standards we Athenians endeavour to live up to in our lives.

Aeschines: But surely Socrates, this goes against the collective folk wisdom of educated people and their common-sense. I feel, and I am sure, that I am solely responsible for all my acts. When I decide to do something, I then carry it out.

Socrates: Are you so sure, my dear fellow? Let us enquire into this matter more closely. Sit down for a while. [My Father and I sit down on some nearby temple steps - to listen to what Socrates had to say] You say "I think", where does the thought that you have, come from, in the first instance? From where does it arise?

Aeschines: From me, of course.

Socrates: From 'me' does it?. Tell us, who is this 'me'? Can you actually find this so called 'me' inside yourself? Now watch closely. Where do these thoughts actually come from? Be very honest Aeschines! Get to know thy Self before it's too late! Tell me Aeschines, have you ever been to Delphi?

Aeschines: Yes, twice.

Socrates: And did you observe what is written somewhere on the temple wall, 'Know Thy Self'?

Aeschines: Yes, Socrates I have seen that aphorism there.

Socrates: Well make the attempt to follow it before it is too late, and you grow old and demented! Now, I repeat have you ever noticed where your thoughts actually come from?

Aeschines: Well, surprisingly they seem to arrive from nowhere, out of the blue. From the Gods, perhaps?

Socrates: Good, now you see that you, your self did not create the initial thought. It arrives from you know not where. Then what happens?

Aeschines: It commences the faculty of reasoning.

Socrates: Yes, it touches your mind, and either the thought is rejected as unworthy or accepted as useful, according to your preferences , your standards of upbringing and so forth; and it starts a process that we call thinking, usually from your associative memory.

Aeschines: But surely I start the process of reasoning?

Socrates: Are you sure, it doesn't just happen? Look closely now. See what actually takes place. A thought arrives from nowhere, touches the mind which reacts according to its patterns of education and conditioning, and does what it believes to be the right response, and some more thought weighs the matter up, and so on, and so on until a conclusion is reached, and action may or may not happen.

Aeschines: But surely in the weighing up, I choose from the possible alternatives offered by commonsense and reason?

Socrates: I mistrust your so called commonsense and conventional opinion, the so-called reason of the masses. Only the philosophers understand the nature of choice, and not too many of them, I suspect.

Aeschines: Do you mean to say I didn't really choose?

Socrates: What happens if you watch, my dear sausage maker, is that your mind or thoughts present alternatives, and according to your disposition you choose that which you consider to be the most practical, pleasurable and in the best interest **for yourself.** But there is no Daemon or entity inside to choose. The choice happens mechanically, like an abacus, and then the mind foolishly ascribes it to itself as "a free agent", boasting arrogantly "I Choose."

Aeschines: Please continue, Socrates. This is most illuminating. [The silent Charinus nods in agreement]

Socrates: Truly the choice was inevitable. The so-called act of choosing was part of the structure of God's will and predetermination. The choice was inevitable, because it appealed to your latent tendencies of pleasure, and what you believe to be appropriate. In fact there was never any freedom to choose anything other than that which was chosen.

Aeschines: But surely if a man does good deeds, they are his own, just as the man who does evil deeds?

Socrates: Again, Aeschines, let us examine very closely. Watch how everything happens. A train of inevitable events leads one man to the good, another to be so-called evil.

Aeschines: How is that?

Socrates: One man is born into a noble womb, with refined, well educated parents, another into a coarse, uncaring home of ignorance. Patterns of behaviour are laid down like a mosaic, by example and imitation. What you call good and bad habits are largely mimicry.

9

Aeschines: But surely, Socrates, there are innate tendencies of good and evil that men are born with?

Socrates: Yes. Souls are transmigrated with these tendencies laid down, inherited from previous lives, and chosen by the Gods for the soul's spiritual development, or shall we say evolution?

Aeschines: So what determines this behaviour of these souls?

Socrates: Examples from parents, family, teachers, people you meet, heroes, reading, inherited characteristics, and so forth. You are conditioned all the time, by each new event, even now, by this conversation, or should I say interrogation?.

Aeschines: So this is this the way the Gods control our destiny?

Socrates: Broadly, yes.

Aeschines: I see. So when I choose, I imagine I'm choosing, but really it's all predetermined.

Socrates: Exactly. You are beginning to see the point.

Aeschines: Then tell me, Socrates, the idea that I can do anything of my own free will, is that falsely imagined?

Socrates: Yes, I am sorry to puncture your vanity.

Aeschines: Then how on earth am I supposed to live?

Socrates: Choose as if you have real choice, knowing, at the back of your mind, that you really have none. This is a step towards inner freedom and the Good. It will remove guilt, and stop you from blaming others for their so called bad deeds, and stop you from flattering others for their so called good deeds, according to society's approval or disapproval. Blaming other people is like blaming doors for banging!

Aeschines: If this was generally understood, what would our Tragedians have to write about?

Socrates: Very little, except trivial comedies like that scurrilous fool Aristophenes. But concerning good and bad, the Nubian, Libyan, Ethiopian, and Egyptian, all have quite different standards from us Greeks, neither better nor worse except according to our opinion. Moreover, each theatrical tragedy should illustrate a flawed characteristic which prevents the hero from coming to Self knowledge. Such was the spiritual blindness of Oedipus for example.

Aeschines: But how can I live, knowing all this effectively?

Socrates: Enjoy yourself, my dear boy. Just be happy. Love your work, and study philosophy, but don't attribute your actions to an imaginary sense of 'me' who doesn't actually exist, that is real slavery.

Aeschines: Thank you Socrates. But...

Socrates: But! There are always 'buts' - listen! This idea that men can act independently of the Gods is at the root of their bondage, and enslaves man and boy alike. To be free, a man must know this clearly. This is my point. I hammer it home continuously.

Aeschines: How am I to see this clearly?

Socrates: Some time in the evening, reflect on the major events of your day and then examine how much they really happened through your own free will? This will undermine your vanity and your pride. Was it your free will that made us almost bump into one another here in Athens this afternoon?

Aeschines: No, Socates, it wasn't, Thank you.

Socrates: The tyrant is the imaginary 'me' who has usurped the Good which is our birthright of freedom. Sacrifice him to the Gods, and all will be well, I promise.

Aeschines: Thank you again, Socrates.

Socrates: Come, my dear friend, let us enjoy your sausages with some finest Chinos wine, here in my flask.

Aeschines: Dear Socrates, my esteemed Master, I cannot find sufficient words with which to thank you enough for this most illuminating conversation. Father and I must hurry back to the shop. We shall be eternally grateful. Fair well, dear friend. [Charinus echoes his son's good byes.]

Chapter 3

A Festive Banquet on Love and Virtue

Characters: Socrates, Callias, Xenophon, Plato, Autolicus, Nicerates, Hermogenes, Phillip (A Comedian), A Syracusian, Chritobulus, Antisthenes, Charmides, Miletus, Lycon, Alciabides, and I.

Like Plato and Xenophon, Aeschines has reported a Symposium on Love and Virtue. His version differs considerably from Plato's which records a different Symposium at which Aeschines was not present. But this Symposium is the same as the one recorded by Xenophon although it differs considerably in style, and substance. Plato was present, made a record, but it was never published. E.R.S.

It was the Festival of the Goddess Athena, the tournament of the Panatheniac Festival had just taken place. Heroic Autolicus was proclaimed the Victor of the Horse Race, and his admirer Callias carried him home, on his broad shoulder, crowned with laurel leaves, along with his father, to his own house in the Piraeum. On the way I met Socrates with Hermogenes, Critobulus, Antisthenes, Alciabides, Charmides, and Miletus, all conversing together, as was their custom.

Callius then generously invited all of us to his house that evening where he promised he would arrange a great celebration with a splendid supper and entertainment. We all accepted, and after returning to our respective homes where we bathed and were anointed, as was customary, we arrived at Callius' palatial Villa and entered the large dining hall. All eyes were attracted by the good looks of the champion Autolicus, and he was praised a great deal for his equestrian triumph. After a sumptuous dinner, accompanied by the finest wine from Chios, a popular comedian called Phillip entered to entertain us. He appeared, acting as if he was uninvited, and asked if he could be seated for supper as he was very hungry. Callias, civil as always, made him feel at home. The fool, anxious to entertain told many ridiculous jokes at which nobody laughed. In despair, Phillip feigned depression, and threw himself down on the nearest couch, covering his head in his cloak and sobbing, while complaining that as there was no more laughter in this world, he might as well be dead! He mimicked being grievously hurt, so Callias consoled him, by saying that we would all try and laugh if only he would eat. Critobulus then burst out laughing which satisfied Philip who proceeded to devour a hearty meal.

Then the entertainment began. After toasting the Gods, a handsome youth and an attractive young girl danced to the accompaniment of a flautist and a harpist. Socrates seemed to be thoroughly enjoying himself and fulsomely thanked Callias for his generous hospitality. Callias asked Socrates if he would like some perfume distributed to complete his evening. This offer Socrates refused adamantly saying that perfumes were unnecessary because of the natural sweetness of all the guests present. Anyway he said that the oil used for rubbing down atheletes appealed to him much more than all the scents used by women and effeminates. "Whether you perfume a slave or a freeman", said Socrates, "it makes no difference to their smell. The odour of honest sweat was always agreeable." [Everyone laughed] Lycon bantered, "this might be pleasant for young men, but for old fogies like he and Socrates, what honest smell would they have?"

Socrates: [quick off the mark, as usual Socrates replied, and the Dialogue began] "The perfume of Virtue and Honour of course, dear friend!"

Lycon: Where do we buy such perfume as you describe Socrates?

Socrates: Not in the shops, I promise you.

Lycon: Where then, indeed?

Socrates: Theognis tell us in his poem [reciting in a mock heroic voice]

When virtuous thoughts warm the celestial mind
With generous heat, each sentiment refined;
The immortal perfume breathing from the heart,
With grateful fragrance, sweetens every part.
But when our vicious passions fire the soul,
The clearest fountains grow corrupt and foul;
The virgin springs which should untainted flow,
Run thick, and darken all the streams below.

[We all applauded Socrates' rendering and then Lycon asked Autolicus if he had understood it?]

Socrates: [interrupting] He not only understands, but he will eventually practice it too. I am confident that when Autolicus comes to contend for virtue and honour he will choose a capable master to instruct him, who will be capable of guiding him to that attainment.

Hermogenes: There is no master I know who is qualified to teach such virtue.

Charmides: Virtue cannot be taught anyway.

Nicerates: If Virtue cannot be taught, then nothing can!

Socrates: Very well, since you cannot agree, let us postpone this topic for the time being, when the right understanding may be present. [I strongly suspected that Socrates was hurt that he was not referred to as the master] Meanwhile let us admire and enjoy the performances of the pretty young dancing girl.

[The girl danced while clashing cymbals, juggling them most skilfully while the handsome youth blew a cheerful tune on his flute and the harpist plucked harmonious chords on her strings.]

There you see that the female sex are not inferior to ours except in the strength of body, and perhaps steadiness of judgement. Those of you who boast wives, take my word for it, they are capable of learning anything you wish that may make them more useful.

Antisthenes: Then why, Socrates, do you not teach Xantippe who appears not to support you?

Socrates: I would never chose a tame horse to teach horsemanship, only a vigorous hard-mouthed one. I now find that with whatever type of person I am with, whatever they say or how disagreeably they say it, it does not disturb my equanimity. This is because I have had the happy opportunity to marry the unhappy hard mouthed one, my beloved Xantippe. [Laughter. Then the nubile dancing girl returned and with the flautist's accompaniment, hurled herself through a hoop of swords with amazing agility. We were all relieved that she did not come to any harm.]

Socrates: Nobody can deny that courage can be learned, and that there are masters in this virtue. None of you here would dare throw yourselves through a hoop of naked swords.

Antisthenes: Truly Socrates, her master could make a fortune by showing her to Athens in the Theatre, and offering them instruction in braving the Lacerdaemonian's steel.

Socrates: It is the unselfconscious, spontaneous living in the present moment, of the wise man, with a completely uncontrived skill in dealing with social and practical matters, which may truly be called Virtue. You have all missed the point.

Antisthenes: Please continue Socrates. You are more interesting than even that handsome flautist and his acrobatic dancing beauty.

Socrates: Superior virtue uses no force, and nothing is left undone to a degree of excellence. Inferior virtue uses unnecessary force but achieves nothing. The ordinary man wants to appear virtuous, and wants to be known as such, but this is not virtue. The naturally virtuous man goes about his necessary affairs, and everything which happens through him is virtuous, because there is no self-interested personal intention or motive left in I him. There is nothing personal he really wants from anybody. All happens serendipitously because he has no sense of an illusory or conceptual personal entity, which I call 'the false sense of me'. He lives happily in the eternal Here and Now. What is false in him has been taken way from him by the grace of the Gods.

Antisthenes: That all sounds very much like some form of Stoicism to me, Socrates.

Socrates: Please let me continue now I am in full flood. Your interruptions are inappropriate. Courageous, virtuous natural living is based on inherent intuition, as distinct from artificial ideas and preconceived notions about what constitutes Virtue. This so called Virtue is imitative and merely based on conditioned, customary rules of social behaviour. It appears to be virtuous behaviour but is probably masking cowardice. Such artificial adherence to custom is usually accompanied by the fear of being misinterpreted in given circumstances and challenges. The Virtue and unpretentiousness of the wise man, which I am talking about, goes unnoticed because of its transparent ordinariness. Now you are all free to interrupt.

Antisthenes: I have nothing to say Socrates. I am lost in admiration for your words of wisdom.

Socrates: Then I shall continue. The virtue of the wise man is not a contrived self-effacement, or self-affliction, like Prodicus and the Stoics practice. Rather it is the annihilation of selfishness in its widest sense. It is neither an assumed humility nor a cloak of hypocrisy which is worn in front of superior authorities like the priests or politicians, and then thrown off. It is closer to the innocent practicality of the cat, a truly virtuous animal if ever there was one. Have you a cat Callias?

Callias: Yes, two Socrates. They keep all the rats at bay, miaow, miaow. The Tom we call Eurymedon and the Tabby we call Eurymedusa!* [laughter].

Eurymedon is the planetary power of Jupiter meaning wise rule and Eurymedusa was King Myrmidon's daughter who was seduced by Jupiter in the form of an ant, and means 'a being of wide cunning'. - E.R.S.]

Charmides: I have a question. Is it possible ever to acquire this Virtue?

Socrates: My dear Charmides. The best way to learn dancing, dear boy, is not by a step to step method but by closely watching with full attention and then when prepared, to get up and follow a dancing master. Why is formal instruction needed to learn swimming? Throw the child in at the deep end and see what happens if he is not already spoiled by his over doting parents. He will surely swim to save his life. Why teach young people to copulate? Put them together stark naked in a bed and then see what happens! [laughter] When wisdom is lost there are pedagogic lectures on and about Virtue. When intellectual knowledge and cleverness enter then very great deceptions arise. When family relations are out of harmony there come all different kinds of ideas about being good parents and being good children. Then the state falls into disorder and misrule, then tyrants come in who say you can trust and rely only on me. [ironic laughter]

Callias: But Socrates....

Socrates: Why does there always have to be a But?... continue if you must.

Callias: Tell me how this squares up with the concept of good and evil in term's of society's laws?

Socrates: From the standpoint of the wisdom of the Sage this question does not arise. The right action is always the spontaneous appropriate action, in the present moment. In the here and now the false sense of any personal 'doership' or 'me', as the sole author of action has gone. He knows the Gods are acting through him, and the question should I, or should I not do this? does not arise. Whatever deed he does, for him is right, because it is the will of the Gods, and he has submitted to that, so he can never act harmfully. Besides so called 'good' and 'evil' are relative terms, merely to describe how a separate ignorant individual, cut off from the Gods, thinks, and responds, like a marionette, to necessary events.

Miletus: Do you ever feel any ill-will, malice, or inward forethought to those puppets Socrates?

Socrates: There is no malice, ill will, or forethought in this body who appears to you as Socrates. How Goodness will work out in a spontaneous, wise action, nobody can foresee. At the moment of action one is merely an instrument of the Good and he or she trusts that force completely. This is faith and virtue combined.

[At that moment following the invitation of Callias the harpist entered again, accompanied by the handsome young flautist. The flautist then put on a graceful exhibition of dancing. There was long applause and shouts of acclamation. Serving boys then entered with flasks of Chios wine and water. They filled the guests' cups in equal measure, as was the custom to preserve sobriety, and departed.]

Socrates: You see this young man, who was good looking enough before, is much more so now he dances well.

Charmides: Come, come, Socrates, now you are talking like a Dancing Master rather than as a teacher of Wisdom.

Socrates: Without doubt, when I see how useful that exercise of dancing is, I come to the veritable conclusion that whoever wishes to keep his or her mind and body in the best of health should definitely learn to dance well. After all this life we live is part of a vast cosmic dance, so many microcosms dancing in the great macosocosm from galaxies to atoms. So let us join in the grand Bacchanalia. As Heraclitus taught us, everything is in a state of flux. I will take a lesson from this Syracusan boy's dancing teacher whenever he so pleases, you can rest assured. Socrates pirouettes in a few graceful steps, to the approval and applause of the company.

[I put down my note taking papyri as I was moved to ask a question.]

Aeschines: Then what advantage will that be to you Socrates, you are already a proficient dancer?

Socrates: Idiot! My advice to you Aeschines is study to know your own Self! while I shall have learned to dance the better for visiting a Dancing Master. [laughter] Have you not heard that when Alciabides came to visit me yesterday morning, he found me dancing?

Alciabiades: I was most impressed Socrates, and now when I heard your arguments, I too shall also take up this recreation. Then perhaps we can both dance together. [laughter].

Charmides: [putting on a pretended air of envy] Please Socrates may I learn to dance with you too?

Socrates: Yes, with all my heart both of you may. Now let us drink a toast to the favoured Divine Terpsichore, the Gods shall bless her.

[All raise their glasses which they drain in one gulp. At a signal from Callias the serving boys re enter and refill their cups with half wine and half water.]

Miletus: I shall sing a song Socrates.

Socrates: By all means Miletus you have a pleasant voice.

Miletus: [singing unaccompanied]

"Oft am I by your women told,

"Poor Socrates! You do grow old;

Look! How your hairs are falling all,

Oh poor Socrates how they do fall!

Whether I'll grow old or no,

By the effects I do not know;

But this I know, without being told,

'Tis time to live, if I grow old;

'Tis time short pleasures now to take,

Of little life the best to make,

And manage well the final stake!"

[applause and laughter]

Socrates: Oh well done, Miletus. Bravo. Even if I do not agree with that Epicurean Philosophy. You are proving a good singer, yes, indeed.

[Prompted by this Phillip the clown rose up from his couch and took Socrates by the hand and they both danced round the room rather awkwardly, obviously in burlesque, and then collapsed on the couch full of laughter.]

Socrates: It is now my wish that we toast this delightful Phillip with wine. The grape moistens the humours and lulls the self-conscious intellect, as laudanum does to the gross, vile body. But if we drink too much or over indulge in opiates, the whole man is deluged and his power of reason is weakened, if not destroyed. But temporally this fine Chios wine distils upon our lungs. As that noble orator and poet Georgias said, "like the sweetest morning dew."

[The serving boys re-enter and carefully refill all the cups with wine mixed with water.]

Charmides: Socrates, what you just said about the wine may also be said about beauty and music. A fine mixture of both drowns sorrow and is the food of love.

Socrates: Very true, Charmides. But I hope now we will make better use of this festive occasion in celebration of Autolicus' victory, for some serious discourse. I shall invite Callias, our bountiful host, to tell us what he learned from his teacher Prodicus, that arch-Stoic, and what he values most?

Callias: Yes, what I value most would be the power to make men be much better than they are.

Antisthenes: How so? Will you make them rich and honest?

Callias: Surely Justice is honesty.

Antisthenes: I agree, Callias, Justice can never mix with dishonesty.

Socrates: We shall return to that proposition presently but first Nicerates, what is the quality you value most ?

Nicerates: It is that my dear father made me learn the whole of Homer by heart! [he recites]

"At last your own death will steal upon you...."

A gentle painless death,
Far from the sea it comes,
To drag you down,
Borne down with the years,
In ripe old age,
With all your people
In blessed peace around you,
All that I have told you will come true."

That's what the Sage Tiresius said in The Odyssey in Book XI line 153 called the Book of the Dead.

Socrates: A bold attempt Niceratus , but you have a long way to go before you can equal my celebrated pupil, the Rhapsodist, Ion. His recitations of Homer are truly inspired, and far better than yours.

Critobulus: Fool! Niceratus, Every street corner entertainer can do what you can do, and they are wretches.

Nicerates: I must agree, they are wretched.

Socrates: Furthermore it is certain they do not understand the meaning of what they recite. Now, Critobulos, what do you value most?

Critobulus: Oh. Beauty, of course.

Socrates: And you Charmides?

Charmides: Poverty.

Socrates: That is the most admirable choice, so far. Even small poverty has it's own security. You may preserve it without any cares, not like the rich, who are in a constant state of frenzied fear and anxiety, in case they lose their wealth, which in the long run they probably shall.

Callias: But what about you, Socrates?

[Then Socrates put on a very grave and solemn expression that set the whole hall laughing.]

I value myself procuring. This will bring in enough money as I please.

[More laughter, and Alcibiades was heard to say Socrates

21

"you pimp."]

Then Lycon addressed the Comic called Philip, and asked what he valued most?

Phillip: Making men laugh of course. Whatever else?

Antisthenes: And how about you Lycon?

Lycon: To be the father of such a noble son as Autolicus.

Miletus: Autolicus no doubt values winning the crown at the Equestrian Races the most.

Autolicus: Not so [blushing] but that I am the son of such a worthy father, is what I value most.

Nicerates: And what about you Hermogenes?

Hermogenes: Virtue, and the bond of friendship.

Miletus: Who are these friends you value so much?

Hermogenes: I will tell you about them in due course.

Socrates: Now, you have all declared your opinions. Please demonstrate them by reason. Callias, you begin.

Callias: I can easily make men just and honest by giving them enough money to fulfill all their needs.

Antisthenes: Is justice found in the heart or in the pocket?

Callias: In the heart. But if they have all the things necessary for a secure life, they will not need to commit any crimes and therefore be honest.

Antisthenes: Will they pay you back?

Callias: Probably not.

Antisthenes: Only with gratitude, perhaps?

Socrates: [interrupts] Anisthenes, I count you among the Cynics.

[Antisthenes ignores the rebuke]

Callias: No, Antisthenes, to answer your question. I have found them generally to be ungrateful. I have even found some wretches who love me less for receiving benefits.

Antisthenes: That is really wonderful. You make them just and honest to others but unjust and dishonest to yourself. Well, well.

Callias: It is not so wonderful. There are architects and masons who live in rented rooms but have the impudent nerve to build palaces for others.

Socrates: Yes, and there are certain diviners who pretend to tell the future but are ignorant of their own fate- that is even worse!

Nicerates: It is now my turn to speak. There is nothing that takes place in this life that the great Homer has not told us about. Whoever would master every quality of heroism and virtue should apply himself zealously to Homer. He shall become educated to perfection. I am entirely master of that science, I assure you.

Antisthenes: Very well. So you have learned the art of Kingship, dear Nicerates, that is all.

Nicerates: [laughing] I learned too how Homer said that an aromatic onion relishes a bottle of wine. Tell a servant to bring an onion to me and we will see with what pleasure we shall drink.

Charmides: Nicerates would rather go home with the smell of an onion on his breath so that his wife may not suspect him of drinking and kissing a wench.

Socrates: An onion not only relishes wine but meat too. Eh, Aeschines you sausage maker? Where we would be without wine and onions? How stupid can we humans be?

Aeschines: Truly yes, that is the case Socrates.

Callias: Onions prepare men for battle. But enough of onions, let us talk about love and beauty. They are more important and less offensive.

Socrates: But they can also drive men and women to tears, alas.

Callias: Yes, Socrates. You too drive us to tears.

Socrates: Enough nonsense! Let us hear from Critobulus.

Critobulus: I shall speak as to why I value myself so much for my handsome good looks. You have all told me that I am vey good looking, and if you derive the same pleasure from looking

23

at me as I do when I see a handsome person, then I would rather be beautiful, both in body and soul, than even be crowned the King of Persia. In truth nothing touches me more than the sight of my dear Kleinias. I would be blind to all other objects if I might always enjoy the sight of my dear Kleinias. Beauty of the human form is generally recognised as superior to all the other attributes, for when she inspires, she makes her votaries both brave and noble. Generals should be the most handsome people in the State.

Socrates: [appearing somewhat irritated] Why for heaven's sake, Critobulus do you allow yourself such absurd airs of vanity? Take due notice, Critobulus that we shall settle this question of beauty in the human form after everyone has his turn to speak.

Hermogenes: Socrates, please do not abandon young foolish Critobulus in this state of mind. The strength of his Narcissism makes me uneasy. Who knows where it may lead?

Socrates: I have observed that he has been like this for some time. His father begged me to cure him. He is better now. I remember once when if Kleinias appeared he would stand up looking as if he was about to be struck down dead. It was as if he had seen the Gorgon Medusa. [laughter]. I remember seeing him run up to poor Kleinias and embrace him wildly. He that would preserve the liberty of his soul must refrain from such strong passions for the snares of either young men or young women.

Charmides: Must we then be afraid of coming too close to such fair people? I remember once when searching in a book you held your head close to Critobulus.

Socrates: Yes, I was punished for that indiscretion for five days. My shoulder felt as if it had been bitten by fierce gnats or stung by fresh nettles, and I felt a sore in my heart. Take note, Critobalus, I would not have you come too close to me dear boy, until you have as many hairs upon your chin as on your head.

Callias: Now Charmides, enough of this frivolity. Tell us what your sound reasons are for your high valuation of Poverty.

Charmides: When I was rich I was in continual fear of being burgled, my goods stolen, and my throat cut into the bargain. Also I was ever besieged by petty fogging, grasping lawyers, book keepers, and wretched beggars who swarm all over Athens like a plague of locusts. They would all try to damage me, one way or another, and I was powerless. I was forced to take high office in the State on my own account and then pay huge taxes for that doubtful privilege. But now that I have divested myself of all my assets I sleep wonderfully well and fearlessly. I am now free, am treated with great respect, and held in esteem by all. I now live like any King, although hopelessly poor, with just enough to feed myself and support a humble lodging. But when I was rich I was in fact a slave. I now have the time and leisure to spend as much time with Socrates as I please, and what could be better than that?! No one takes advantage of me, because I have nothing for them to take or lose.

Callias: So you plead eloquently against the disease of riches. How exceptional you are.

Socrates: Antisthenes, why, as you are poor, do you also put little value on wealth?

Antisthenes: I believe that what we term 'rich' or 'poor', are really qualities in the heart. I feel great compassion for all those who are slaves to their wealth. They can never be satisfied, always desiring more and more. I live very simply, not possessing more than I need for simple food and lodging. In my view, it is necessary to live this way in order to live honestly. The only true wealth I possess is that wisdom given to me by Socrates. He never measures his gifts but bestows as much knowledge as I can assimilate whenever I need it. I am now the master of my leisure, and I can hear him from morning to night. Who could be richer than that?

Callias: I admire you greatly, my friend.

Nicerates: Please do not envy Antisthenes too much. I am about to quote from Homer, for by reading him I have realised in the Bard's own words:

"Ten golden talents, seven three legged stools,
Just twenty cisterns, and twelve charging steeds."

This passage has made me always to be numbering, that I am afraid I am mistaken for a miser. [laughter]

Socrates: I would ask Xenophon or Aeschines what they would like to say, but they are both much too busy scribbling. I trust they will be accurate unlike that young Plato over there. Now tell us Hermogenes, about the great value you place upon friends and friendship.

Hermogenes: It is universally recognised amongst the barbarians as well as the Greeks that the Gods know what lies in the present moment, and what is yet to come. So they are consulted and applied to by all mankind, and worshipped with sacrifices and prayers to pacify their will. So we must be friends of the Gods and value their friendship with us.

Socrates: Surely, Hermogenes, you can see that the will of the Gods is constantly unfolding in all that is happening, here and now, at this very moment. The 'now' is 'what is', and therefore must be the will of the Gods. The future is its certain unfoldment. If men fully accepted this, they would not need to make so many prayers and sacrifices. All happens for the best, as 'what is' is the preordained, prescribed will of the Gods. Man's task is to will 'what is' and their own destiny too. Then they can rest in total harmony and acceptance of the will of the Gods. When they strive and rage against the Gods like poor wretched Prometheus, they suffer interminably. They should not pit themselves against the will of the Gods in thought or deed. Here lies the true path of virtue and happiness. The other way is arrogance, pride and hubris. It ends in tragedy, as we all well know from the Theatre.

Hermogenes: Thank you Socrates. Does this also mean that what the Gods will is always virtuous and must be the Good?

Socrates: Yes. There is no other basis for the Good. Man cannot always see at the time that what is happening is for the universal Good, for the absolutely necessary cosmic balance and harmony for the Whole, because sometimes it seems to damage him personally. What we think may be bad, doesn't always work out to be so. Later we see that it was a blessing wrapped up in a cloak. We cannot understand the Higher Wisdom. Later, well after the event, we may see the lesson contained in the event, and be truly grateful. We must, however, submit to what happens, accepting all that unfolds gracefully. This is the key. All your tragedies in life and in the theatre come about because of non-acceptance of the will of the Gods. Not my petty little ant-like will, but the Gods omnipotent will, let that will be done, I say. This is the beginning and end of the virtuous life.

Hermogenes: Yes, I have always supposed that the Gods have the power to do to us what is truly Good. So these very Gods, who are all-seeing, and all-knowing are all-powerful as well. I believe that they are my friends and so take care of me and guard me, whatever happens.

Socrates: This is the beginning of faith and wisdom. Although we talk of many Gods to distinguish their functions, they are all really aspects of the ultimate One Good, from which all life springs. The One Good speaks to you and teaches you through the situation in which he places you in, at any one moment. Be watchful and observe!

Hermogenes: Yes, Socrates, we are in full agreement here. The Good informs us and forewarns us by its secret presence, hidden in the innermost core of our very being. We have to listen to that which speaks out of silence, in which the Good's voice is revealed. Our petty selfishness and inner turmoil obscures its message. We must bravely struggle against vanity and pride. Sometimes a vivid dream will inform us of the future and the action we must follow. The Oracle is in touch with the will of the Gods and can inform us.

Socrates: Very good. There is nothing that you have said with which I could disagree. I would be pleased to hear by what means you oblige the Gods to befriend you so well.

Hermogenes: I return grateful thanks at all occasions, for whatever happens, whether my poor mind thinks that it is either good or bad. Then my will is the same as the will of the Gods, so all is ultimately good and well.

Socrates: Truly, if such men as you have the Gods as friends, and I am sure you have, like I have; it is certain that these Gods are pleased that good and noble deeds are being fulfilled by you, through the practice of Virtue.

Hermogenes: So it follows that if I wish to know the will of the Good, it is what is actually happening now, Socrates?

Socrates: Precisely Hermogenes! If all men and women were as perceptive as you are, we would have less inner conflict, unnecessary suffering and wretched misery. Welcome wholeheartedly what is happening inside and outside the skin. That is what is needed to become an inwardly free and happy man or woman. Yes Hermogenes you see the Good is Love. The Self of each being is Love. Don't obscure it with fear, greed, anger, envy, hatred, worry and anxiety. Cleanse yourself of these ignoble tendencies! Let Love or the Self take over your life. She wants to consume you in her fire, so you will rise as the Egyptians say, like a Phoenix. Don't refuse the divine will.

Hermogenes: I try not to reject it, but sometimes when I suffer or see other people suffering, I ask is this really the God of Love?

Socrates: My dear boy, where would we be without our suffering? It is the play of Love to bring us closer to her. The hardness of heart, our selfish pride, and self-will shields us from Love's entreaties. We are unaware she is ever inviting us on all occasions, at every moment, to be one with us. We resist her by our false sense of individuality, so she cannot touch us except by showing us her healing power and new direction, after we suffer some blow of fate.

Hermogenes: Yes but....

Socrates: Yes, Hermogenes, but.... You are always full of buts. Just let go of the buts and bathe in the Love of your own true Self, the source of your own being. Enquire within scrupulously and persistently, seek her out, until your obscuring arrogance topples. Let Love have an affair with you. She will woo you, seduce you, and after once tasting her embrace, you will never want to leave her again and always grieve her absence. That is the real marriage, then you as Love, your true nature, are forever united with the one God of Love. You are at blissful peace. Is that clearer now?

Hermogenes: Yes, I am truly grateful Socrates. Thank you.

Socrates: So trust Love, all of you! She is the Mother Goddess, She will look after you, take care of you and gently lead you to Self Knowledge and inner peace. Sometimes She appears to give you a rough ride, Her route is often through difficult country, before She drops you safely at home. Never wilt or be disheartened, trust Her, She is full of kindness and grace,.She will never let you down, in spite of what you imagine life is doing to you at the moment.

Hermogenes: I suppose Socrates, we don't trust enough. I am often afraid that things are not going to work out for the best.

Socrates: Fear is our greatest enemy. It prevents Love from entering into our awareness and our hearts. Never, ever fear, everything works out perfectly in the long run even if in the short term it seems to look disastrous. Even the so-called disasters are blessings in fancy dress. They are the harbingers of Love's arrival.

Hermogenes: Thank you Socrates.

Socrates: Why people do not have the humility to accept that they are shadow puppets in a cave, in the hands of the Gods, is beyond me.

Hermogenes: But what can I do to ameliorate the sufferings of other people Socrates?

Socrates: You can do very little. But if it happens that when suffering crosses your path, and there is the possibility of relieving it, and your heart is open with compassion, you will do all you can to help a poor suffering fellow creature. Help whenever you can, but stop agonising about situations in which you are powerless. Every one has a preordained fate, which the Gods have prepared for each one's spiritual development. So it is all based on Love. There is no death. The soul is reborn into another life, after so-called death, to continue its journey to eventual Self Knowledge, bliss and peace.

Hermogenes: Thank you Socrates. Is all this what men call Grace?

Socrates: Yes mercy and grace are all linked with Love. Let your tears of gratitude wash away the dark dirt of ignorance obscuring your own dear Self which is Love.

Charmides: So Love has nothing to do with lust then?

Socrates: No! Lust is from the selfish false sense of a 'me' desperate for some pleasurable, momentary relief from its anguish and boredom. Love is refined, and her amorous advances are from the spirit, not the body. Remember that Charmides.

Charmides: That is a revelation Socrates.

Socrates: Now Miletus, please sing us a song about Love-bring on the flautist and harpist too.

Miletus sings:
Love that is first and last of all things made,
The light that has the living world for shade,
The spirit that for temporal veil has on
The souls of men, all woven in blessed unison.
One fiery raiment with all lives inwrought,
And lights of sunny, starry deed and thought,
And always through each act and passion new,
Shines the divine same form and beauty through.
The body spiritual of fire and light
Is to worldly noon as noon to night.

Love, that is flesh upon the spirit of man
And spirit within the flesh whence breath began;
Love that keeps all the choir of lives in chime;
Love, that is blood within the veins of time.
So strong that heaven, could love bid heaven fairwell,
Would turn to fruitless and unflowering hell;
So sweet that hell, to hell could love be given,
Would turn to splendid and sonorous heaven.
Love that is fire within you and light above,
And lives by grace of nothing but true love.

Miletus: Now let us all sing the last two lines together...

Love that is fire within you and light above
And lives by grace of nothing but true love.

[All sing together, then cheer and applaud Miletus]

Socrates: Callias, please can we have more wine, our throats are parched after all that singing and cheering.

[Callias summons the serving boys who bring in more flasks of wine and water refilling the cups of the guests in equal measure.]

Socrates: Thank you Miletus, that song was really worthy of the occasion. [Socrates warmly embraces Miletus]

Now let us change the topic and ask Phillip what he finds so valuable in his profession?

Phillip: I am very proud of my craft as a comedian. All Athens knows I am a buffoon. If good fortune happens to them they invite me to entertain them When misfortune comes.....

[Socrates interrupts]

Socrates: Is it really misfortune- but not a blessing in masked costume sent from the Gods?

Phillip: If they believe they have suffered misfortune, according to their lights, they avoid me like the plague, lest I should succeed in making them laugh, in spite of their wretched little selves which love wallowing in misery. [laughter]

Charmides: Syracusian, [the owner of the slave dancing girl and boy] on what do you value yourself? I suppose it is that girl of yours or is it the boy?

Syracusian: Neither. But I am fearful about the attempts of some people to try and ruin them.

Socrates: Ah! What possible wrong could these innocent children suffer from them? Do they wish to kill them Syracusian? No. Or go to bed with them? Suppose that happened, would this ruin them? Do you not rest with them yourself?

Syracusian: Yes, all night long.

Socrates: By Hera, you are a happy rogue to be the only man in the world that doesn't ruin those you go to bed with. Your pride is that you are harmless and wholesome as a bedfellow.

Syracusian: You are wrong Socrates. I value myself for the fact that there are so many fools in the world who come to see my children dance and so supply me with the necessities of life.

Phillip: I suppose that was why I heard you pray the other day?

"Immortal Beings grant my humble prayer;

Give Athens all the blessings you can dispense

Let them abound in plenty, peace and pence."

Callias: This is all very well, but Socrates, what possible reason have you to make us believe that you are fond of the very profession you claimed, that of Procurer? I think that is absolutely scandalous! Are you some kind of philosophical pimp? [laughter]

Socrates: [quite unperturbed] Let us very clearly understand each other. I wish to tell you in a few words what I, as a Philosopher, am properly to do, whose very name has made you all happy. So briefly, let us in short, fix on just one thing that we may all agree with, shall we?

All: Yes!

Socrates: Is it not true that the business of a Philosopher is to be perfectly agreeable to whom ever employs him?

All: Yes!

Socrates: Is it not certain too that a noble countenance and good clothes, both contribute towards making such a person agreeable to you?

All: Yes!

Socrates: Do you not observe that his eyes look sometimes full of kindness, at other times full of scorn and often full of a penetrating gaze.?

All: Yes! [enjoying the fun]

Socrates: Does not his voice sometimes express itself modestly and sweetly, and sometimes with anger and fierceness?

All: Yes!

Socrates: Do not some discourses naturally beget aversion and others love and affection?

All: Yes!

Socrates: If then the Philosopher be excellent in his profession ought he not to instruct those under his direction which way to make them also agreeable in every other way too?

All: Yes!

Socrates: But who is the most valued? Surely he who renders them agreeable not only to one person, but to many.

All: Yes!

Socrates: But what if the Philosopher can instruct his pupil to gain the hearts of a whole Greek State? Will you not say that he is excellent in his profession?

All: Yes! [mixed with some sceptical laughter]

Socrates: If he can raise his pupils to such perfection has he not good reason to be proud of his profession, doesn't he deserve a decent reward?

All: Yes! [more laughter]

Socrates: Now, if there is such a man to be found in the whole world it is Antisthenes- or am I mistaken?

Antishenes: How, Socrates, will you make me one of your scurvy philosophers?

Socrates: Certainly, for I know you are perfectly skilled as a

Procurer.

Antisthenes: Did you ever know me of being guilty of such a heinous deed?

Socrates: Yes, Antisthenes, please relax. You procured Callias for Prodicus, finding the one who was in love with Philosophy, and the other in want of cash. You did the same for Hippias, who taught him the skill of good memory, and consequently has become more lustful than ever. Whenever he sees a good looking man or woman he cannot forget him or her for a moment. What is more, when you praised Heraclea, it made me want to meet him too. I found him a very worthy man indeed. Similarly you praised Esquilus to me, and me to him, and inflamed us both with such a desire to meet each other, so that we searched Athens every day until the meeting took place. Thus, I have deduced that you are an excellent Procurer, a 'bringer of people together'. Maybe you will soon be capable of bringing about the near impossible agreement between the different Greek States? [laughter] Yet, you showed anger when I said you were a Procurer.

Antisthenes: That is true, Socrates. My anger has, however, calmed, and I am comforted that I must posses a soul which is incomparably rich like yours, and a Procurer of good souls like your good self.

Nicerates: Now, Critobulus, will you not dare dispute this question of true beauty with Socrates?

Socrates: I don't believe he will, for he knows my profession as a philosopher attracts too much interest from the jealous Magistrates.

Critobulus: I shall enter the lists. Now dear Socrates, use all your gifts of eloquence and persuasion to prove that you are handsomer and more beautiful than I am. [laughter]

Socrates: Do you really believe Critobulus, that beauty is nowhere to be found but in the human body?

Critobulus: Yes, certainly, it is found in other creatures

34

whether animate, like a horse, a bull, or a cat, or inanimate things like swords, shields, vases, sculptures and so on.

Socrates: Good. Now tell me how it is that things which are so very different should all appear to be handsome and beautiful?

Critobulus: Because they are all well fashioned either by Nature or Art and their underlying substratum is the very force of life itself, I suppose you could call it Consciousness, that is what you once taught me, did you not?

Socrates: Excellent, Critobulus. Now do you know the use of the eyes?

Critobulus: To see, of course.

Socrates: Well that is the very reason that mine are handsomer than yours.

Critobulus: Give me your reason for that statement, please.

Socrates: Your eyes see only in a direct line, but with mine I can look not only directly forward as you can, but sideways too, for they are seated on a jutting ridge on my face and can stare out sideways as well. [laughter]

Critobulus: At that rate a crab has the most beautiful eyes of all creatures.

Socrates: I agree for they are sited more suitably than many other creatures.

Critobulus: Be that as it may with the eyes, but as for noses, could you possibly make me believe that your ugly proboscis is more beautiful than mine?

Socrates: There is no room for a shadow of a doubt! As the Gods fashioned noses for smelling and breathing, your nostrils face downwards, but mine are wide and are turned upwards towards Elysium. I receive odours and breezes which flow from all parts of the universe, above and below. [laughter]

Critobulus: What! Is a short, flat, snub nose more beautiful than a well shaped one like mine?

Socrates: Of course! Because being short and flat, it never hinders the sight of both eyes at once. Your high nose parts the eyes so much that it hinders the possibility of you seeing anything directly, clouded by your pink fuzz.

Critobulus: On that utilitarian, rather than aesthetic basis, I grant that your mouth is much more beautiful than mine, because it is capable of eating three times as much as mine at the same time.

Socrates: Than my kisses must be much sweeter and more fulfiling than yours, because my lips are much larger and more fulsome?

Critobulus: So a donkey's lips are more beautiful than mine then? [laughter]

Socrates: Finally, I look much more like the beautiful Sileni than you do, and they come from the Naiades, the sea Goddess, so there! [much laughter]

Critobulus: It is obviously impossible to dispute with you Socrates. I pray we take good note, and test by ballot in the dark, so that your eloquence doesn't corrupt the company even more. [laughter from all including Socrates whose sides shake with mirth]

[At that moment from a signal by Callias the little dancing boy and girl ceremoniously enter carrying a ballot box and Socrates asked for the candles to be snuffed out, and for a torch to be held in front of Critobulus, so that the judges might not be surprised by their judgement. Socrates declared that the winner instead of a garland or wreath should receive a kiss from everyone of the company instead. They then voted and it went unanimously to Critobulus whereupon Socrates roared with laughter and said....]

Socrates: Critobulus, your money has not the same effect as Callias on beggars to make them more just, for yours I see can corrupt all the judges upon the bench! [laughter]. Critobulus, you must demand your kisses, as a due reward for your victory. Everyone laughed more loudly than ever. They all submitted except for Hermogenes who appeared to be bashfully reticent.]

Socrates: Tell me Hermogenes, do you know the meaning of the word paranoia?

Hermogenes: I will give you my opinion, but I am not sure if it is the exact meaning.

Socrates: Please continue.

Hermogenes: I believe that paranoia signifies the irrational and exaggerated fear we feel in the presence of others.

Socrates: That, Hermogenes, is the reason for your shyness.

Hermogenes: No one can get away with anything with you around Socrates.

Socrates: Can you help him Callias?

Callias: Yes, I propose that when the entertainment starts that everyone must shut up including the bashful Hermogenes. [laughter]

Hermogenes: You would consign me to the same pathetic plight as Nicostates who used to recite his Homer to the sound of a flute. It would be charming if I could address you all to the accompaniment of music.

Socrates: For goodness sake do so, dear boy. The harmony is most agreeable when voice and instruments perform well together. Your speech will no doubt be much more entertaining. Perhaps you could gesture a little as the young girl does when she plays her flute?

Callias: But when Antisthenes is content to be angry in company, what flute will ever be tuneable to such a voice?

Antisthenes: I have no idea when there will be occasion for flutes to be tuned to my vocal chords, but I know when I am cross, as I am more than loud enough. What is more important is to know that the melody represents the soul in music.

Syracusian: Are you by any chance that same Socrates nicknamed 'The Contemplative'? Aristophenes satirizes you in his play called The Clouds, doesn't he?

Socrates: Yes, rather badly; I fear for his reputation.

Charmides: Oh Socrates, when I heard his words I was doubled up with laughter.

Socrates: Please tell us.

Charmides: [pulling out a sheet of text from his robe]

"Oh you who would high wisdom attain,

Socrates comes in our direst need.

To all Greeks around, his glories resound.

Such a prosperous life, you shall lead.

You'll be blest with a memory that's good,

And accustomed profoundly to think,

And your soul ignore all needs to endure,

And from no undertaking ever shrink.

You're hardy and bold to bear up against cold,

With forbearance, your supper you lose,

You no more incline to gymnastics or wine,

And all lusts of your body refuse.

You esteem it best, which is always the test

To claim a truly intelligent brain,

To prevail and succeed whenever you plead,

And power of tongue in conquests to gain.

But as far as a sturdy soul is concerned.

With its horrible restless care

And a belly that pines and wears away,

On the wretchedest, frugalest fare,

You may hammer and strike as long as you like;

You are quite invincible there!"

[loud applause and clapping]

[Socrates rises and takes a bow holding Charmides' hand who also bows.]

Socrates: Well recited dear Charmides.

Charmides: Did you enjoy the play Socrates?

Socrates: I laughed at myself occasionally, but fundamentally it is a false portrayal of my vocation.

Charmides: In what respect?

Socrates: Well, no true Philosopher would ever teach a debtor how to dissemble. My pupils flock to me because they desire to know the Truth. The Gods select them and me as vehicles to convey this enlightenment.

Charmides: That sounds most elitist and vain, Socrates.

Socrates: It not only may sound so, it actually is the case. But there is one good hymn in Aristophenes' play. A prayer which quite moved me. I have learned it by heart. [He recites]

"Almighty God, oh heavenly King
First unto Thee my prayer I bring,
Oh hear, Lord Zeus, my choral song;
Thou, dread power, whose resistless hand
Heaves up the sea and trembling land.
Lord of the trident, stern and strong,
Thou who sustains the life of all,
Celestial Ether, Father, come to my call!
Thou who floods the world with light,
Guiding steeds through the glittering sky,
For men below and to gods on high
A true Potentate heavenly-bright!"
[loud applause and cheers]

Now that is reasonably good Poetry, not the comic rubbish that foolish playwright usually dishes up, alas. Now, good Syracusan, what were you saying?

Syracusan: They say Socrates, that you only contemplate the sublime?

Socrates: Yes, can you envisage anything more sublime in the universe so sublime as the One Good and the Self-Existent?

Syracusan: But I am told that your contemplations are not in that direction, but ever so trifling, and that in stretching enquiries beyond your reach, your contemplations amount to absolutely nothing.

Socrates: It is by contemplation and this enquiry that I attain to the knowledge of the Good , which is synonymous with Self

Knowledge when all is understood to be One. The inner and outer merge into Unity, and an ineffable state of bliss reveals the All. If what I say seems dry and inspid for you, it is because you yourself are dry and insipid.

Syracusan: [hastily] Let us change the topic Socrates. How far can a flea skip? They say you are also a subtle mathematician and understand Geometry well.

Antisthenes: [interrupting] Please, Phillip you are good at making comparisons. Who is this impudent Syracusan really like.

Phillip: Yes, he strikes me as insolent too, like a bad new wine which pretends to be a grand vintage.

Socrates: Careful! Do not insult him less you fall under the same disposition that you attribute to him.

Phillip: Suppose I compare him with a true aristocrat then?

Socrates: Comparisons always have a bad odour. Compare him with nobody.

Phillip: That is true. I suppose it is better to remain silent then say something we ought not to say.

Socrates: Now enough of this nonsense. Let us sing our anthem together, those who remember it, Nicerates certainly will. It's from the immortal Homer. [most join in, and the dancing girl and the boy flautist enter carrying a potter's wheel which they daintily trip around, as he plays his flute along with the harpist who has also entered.

"Let men their days in senseless strife employ,
We rest in eternal peace and constant joy.
Thou Mother Goddess, with our Sire comply,
Nor ever break the sacred union of the sky;
Lest roused to rage, He shakes the blest abodes,
Launch red lightning, and dethrone the gods.
If you submit, the Thunderer stands appeased'
The gracious power is ever willing to be pleased."

Socrates: [recovering his breath] I earnestly believe I shall now pass for a contemplative person for I am now meditating how it happens that these two little dancers give us so much pleasure. But such questions are not really proper at this time. Perhaps we would enjoy them more if they were to dance 'The Four Season' dressed as nymphs? [laughter]

Syracusan: You are quite right Sir. I will now go and rehearse them in something more suitable for them to perform at this noble feast: and I apologise for my rudeness. In truth you are a wise man.

Socrates: [rising to his full height] What then, must we disperse without saying a word of the attributes of that great Daemon, spirit or power who is palpably present here and equals in age the eternity of the Gods ,although to look at He resembles a child? That spirit who by His mighty power is master of all things, and is also grafted onto the very essence and constitution of man's soul [he paused for effect]..... I mean Love! We may with our entire reason praise his domain as we have more knowledge of its power than the common folk who are not initiated into the mysteries of that great God as we are. For myself, I never can remember when I was without being in love. I know, too, that Charmides shares my experience and Critobulus no doubt shall. Nicerastes loves his wife, and his Homer passionately, and this love is reciprocated by her. Hermogenes loves honesty and virtue intensely. You can see and feel it in his presence. He is loved by his friends the Gods, and he does not despise his poor fellow mortals. But as for you Antisthenes, are you the only one in this gallant company who does not love?

Antisthenes: No, for I love you, Socrates with all of my heart. [Socrates feigns embarrassment]

Socrates: Do not please trouble me with that now, you see I have other work on my hands.

Antisthenes: I confess you must be an expert master of that pimping art with which you valued yourself so much a little while ago. Sometimes you are at great pains to talk with me, sometimes you say your Daemon will not allow you, or that you have other things to do.

Socrates: Spare me, Antisthenes. I can well bear any troubles you put on me, but I tremble to speak of your passion for me which is for the bodily form you see here, and not for my immortal soul. As for you, my Callias, you, as well as the rest of us, and especially Autolicus, along with the whole of Athens, know that the real reason you love him, is because you both descend from illustrious families, and each of you possess excellent qualities which make you both even more illustrious. I have always admired the sweetness of your temper, and your love for Autolicus is for a truly virtuous soul. I confess that I am not firmly convinced whether there be one Aphrodite, the Goddess of Beauty and Love, or two. The celestial and the vulgar. It may be that with this Goddess, it is the same as with Zeus, who has many names, but there is still only one Zeus. But I know that both Aphrodites have different altars, temples and sacrifices. The vulgar Aphrodite is worshiped often in a very negligent and tasteless manner, whereas the celestial one is adored for her purity and sanctity of life. The vulgar inspires mankind with the love of the body only, but the celestial fires the mind with the love of the immortal soul and Being. It leads to a friendship and a genuine thirst after noble deeds. I trust and hope that it is this last kind of love which has touched your heart! I believe that your love is wholly virtuous, for whenever you wish to converse with him, it is in the presence of his father. This shows that your love is honourable. The Higher Love I am speaking about is when the personal, petty, little sense of 'me' is totally absent, and then the pure love which is our true nature flows effortlessly. Everything we see and touch is loved by us, because we know it to be divine in essence. When this false sense of the petty little 'me' is there I am in a love divided between myself as the subject and the perceived object. Then the desire for possessiveness arises too easily. So all of you, I am instructing you to disappear as petty little 'me's' and allow this purified love to invade your whole being unconditionally!

Hermogenes: I have always greatly admired you dear Socrates, but much more now, than ever before, for pointing out to us the true nature of Love.

Socrates: That is the case, and I shall now prove to you that this pure love is incomparably superior to the mere love or adoration of one's own body or another's. We can observe that all those who admire the bodily form of an individual, almost to the point of worship, only disapprove of that person after they have attempted and failed to possess that body. Even if there is a strong mutual passion between the two as lovers, it is certain that when the power of beauty decays and perishes, then the love built on such a foundation cannot be sustained. Lust is not the same as true love, it's obviously its opposite. With the Soul or Self or Being, the more that it ripens, she or he, eventually becomes the embodiment of love. Also remember that the Good, and the God who is One, are all Love. It is like I have found out, that if one continually indulges in consuming rich delicacies it leads to disgust, just as the continuous consumption of sexual consummation leads to disgust as well [mild laughter and some nodding of heads]. Yet that love that fastens on the soul's shining qualities, or being, or character, becomes more and more brilliant as time goes on. Furthermore if love is pure and chaste it never tires. All prayers are answered. It is unnecessary to prove that a man or woman of noble qualities, held in high esteem, must infallibly return the love that is bestowed upon him. How can it happen otherwise but that persons who love one another, in this way, tenderly, with all the freedom of a pure and sacred friendship, will derive the utmost satisfaction in each other's company and share everything together. This is happiness. This contrasts vividly with those who love out of bodily attraction alone. Why should he or she who loves only external beauty continue with that passion indefinitely? This love is based on gaining pleasure for the false sense of 'me' which lasts for a ridiculously short time. True love is based on the irreversible sacrifice of the false sense of 'me' for the sake of the Good and the Beloved.

So Callias you are infinitely obliged to those Gods who have inspired in you a true love and friendship for Autolicus. Autolicus has proved his capacity to overcome hardship by his prowess in athletics and horsemanship. I know this discourse has been too serious for a banquet, but I have always wished to encourage those of virtuous disposition, and help others to find it. It is surely time for a Song. Miletus please lighten our mood, and honour us with one of your musical lyrics.

Miletus: Certainly Socrates, for I love you just as you describe. [He reaches for a lyre next to him on his couch and announces...] This song is dedicated to the humble Grasshopper. [he sings]

Happy insect! What can be
Real happiness compared to thee?
Fed with nourishment divine,
The dewy morning's gentle wine.
Nature waits upon thee still
And thy verdant cup does fill;
'Tis filled wherever thou dost tread,
Nature's Self, thy Ganymede.
Thou dost drink, and dance, and sing;
Happier than the happiest King!
All the grass which thou dost see,
All God's plants belong to thee.
Thou dost innocently all things enjoy;
Nor does any luxury thy soul destroy;
The shepherd gladly heareth thee,
Thou art more harmonious than even he.
To thee, of all things upon earth,
Life's no longer than thy mirth.
Happy insect, so blessed thou

44

Dost neither age nor winter know.

But when thou'st drunk, danced and sung

Thy fill, the flowery leaves among.

Sated with the summer's zest

Thou retires to endless rest.

[applause]

Socrates: Bravo! fair Miletus.

Callias: You must always support me with your inestimable wisdom, Socrates.

Socrates: You shall certainly triumph? Never doubt it. You must apply yourself earnestly to the study of virtue and not be contented with only its appearance as many do. False glory can never endure for long. Flattery and praise may serve a mouldering edifice for a time, but it must ultimately collapse in ruins. True Virtue, however, will always maintain its reign. Sublime Virtue rest well on the man who exhibits it, his face beams with rays of glory that shine brighter and brighter as his virtuous qualities mature and flourish. [Socrates paused. There was a long silence, after which Socrates rose and the party began to disband.]

Autolicus: Before we go I must declare to all the assembled company that I find you Socrates, a virtuous and honourable man, the epitome of true love. [There was general acclamation. Then as a closing ceremony the Syracusan brought in an elaborately carved chair, sat down and spoke.]

Syracusan: Gentleman. Ariadne is about to enter and Bacchus who has been drinking with the Gods is coming here to accompany her. [The girl dancer entered dressed in a whie bridal costume and sat down in the chair vacated by the Syracusan. Then the flautist dressed up as Bacchus, in a goatskin jacket, and a headpiece of horns, played a sweet melody on his flute accompanied by the harpist. Then he sat down on Ariadne's lap and kissed her. She returned his embrace.]

Bacchus: Do you truly love me, my dearest one?

Ariadne: Yes, yes, my beloved. Let me perish if I fail to love thee from the goodness of my heart for ever.

Both together: Adieu good folks , parctice true love and virtue for tomorrow we die.

There was loud applause for the actors, then for Callias for hosting such a memorable Banquet The players and the Syracusan were all warmly thanked. Everyone prepared to go their separate ways. I left with Socrates as a beautiful golden dawn slowly broke over the Acropolis.

Chapter 4

Ion or The Iliad - The Rupturing of a Rhapsodist's Pride

Introduction

No historical record exists that Aeschines ever recorded the Socratic Dialogue entitled Ion or the Iliad, named after Ion the Poet, who was its main character, and the Iliad, that great work of Homer, concerning the Trojan War, to which this dialogue occasionally quotes. Nor is Aeschines included in the list of participants named by Plato. He may well have been excluded from Plato's report, although he could well have been there, because of the known jealousy and antagonism which existed between these two Scribes. This is the most probable explanation for this regrettable lacuna that exists in Socratic scholarship. Nevertheless good fortune has led me to discover this magnificent Socratic Dialogue, called Ion or the Iliad, on the topic of Poetry, also transcribed by Aeschines. I am pleased to present my tentative translation to all those who either study or admire the wisdom of the legendary Socrates, in which he displays his masterly skill in the art of ruthless cross examination. Aeschines' account is much readable, more dramatic and entertaining than Plato's in my opinion. In my first translation, that of the Banquet, we see Socrates at his wittiest and most amusing, and sometimes at his wisest and most profound. Here, as a contrast, we see the full display of his masterly skill as a serious dialectician with a moral purpose.

Earnest Sekers

Ion or the Iliad

Characters: Socrates, Ion, Aeschines and Plato.

The Dialogue takes place in the house of Socrates. The Poet Ion had been invited a long time ago, to call upon him whenever he is moved to do so, as he regards himself as a pupil of the Master.

Socrates: Hail, fair Ion! A hearty welcome my dear boy,!where are you coming from to be back among us once more? From your beautiful homeland of Ephesus, no doubt?

Ion: No, my dear Socrates, I have just returned from the great festival in honour of Asclepius at Epidarus.

Socrates: Ah! Did the Epidaurians hold a contest of leading Rhapsodists* in honour of the great God?

A Rhapsodist in Ancient Greece was an itinerant public performer of Poetic recitation or declamation. His role was partly educational, and partly theatrical. It usually applied to the ecstatic, unrestrained, enthusiastic performance of an Epic, such as those of Homer, or a long string of favourite Poems by popular Greek authors. - E.R.S.

Ion: Yes, Socrates, and the contests were not among Rhapsodists alone, there were many competitions in various kinds of music and poetry.

Socrates: And which contest did you compete in, and how successful were you, Ion?

Ion: [proudly puffing up his chest] Well, I easily won first prize at the Rhapsodist contest, Socrates. It was not a surprise, the other competitors were all mediocre.

Socrates: Heartiest congratulations, my dear boy, well done!, you have now only to plan how to win the Panathenaea.

Ion: That will undoubtedly happen if God is willing, Socrates.

Socrates: To enjoy the profession of a Rhapsodist, Ion, has often seemed to me to be a most enviable one. For it combines taking care of your mind, body and spirit along with scrupulous elegance of dress. It means that you have to carefully study most of our excellent Greek Poets and especially our magnificent Homer. It is not only because you have to memorise his works well, but because, without a doubt, you have also to understand his innermost thoughts. For he is not worthy of the name of Rhapodist who does not familiarise himself well, with the whole scope and intention of any Poet whom he is privileged to recite, and be capable of transmitting that understanding to his attentive public.

Ion: That is perfectly correct Socrates. Indeed I have made an earnest effort to accomplish this skill and have acquired a complete scientific knowledge of Homer, and of all that constitutes great poetry. When I practice my Profession. I am second to none, in this respect. I am convinced that there is nobody in this world more capable, in the interpretation of Homer, and better able to express his beautiful verses, than I. Not even Metrodorus, Stesimbrotus, Glauco, or any other so called contemporary Rhapsodist.

Socrates: I am more than convinced, my dear Ion, that you have considerable ability as a Rhapsodist, otherwise you could not win so many prizes. I hope you will be so kind as to recite for me some day.

Ion: Yes, Socrates. It would be well worth your time to come and hear me recite Homer. I have considerably influenced your pupil Niceratus, as you probably know. Sometimes I feel I deserve a crown of gold from my great number of admirers.

Socrates: Yes Ion, [sarcastically] modesty was always your strongest point. I will find the time some day to hear you declaim. But now I wish to ask you some very important questions. I have invited dear Aeschines and Plato to be here, and endeavour to record what I intend to be an instructive Dialogue with you, my dear boy. Neither of them arealways accurate, but hopefully, if we put the two versions together, we may have some clear summary of the points I intend to make and what follows from them. Aeschines is often crude in his recording, and Plato does not always report what I actually said, for reasons best known to himself. I suspect he has his own ambitions for the future [Plato blushes]. By the way did you bring any of your delicious sausage meats with you, my good Aeschienes?

Aeschines: It is most kind of you to invite us, Socrates but regrettably our shop has sold out of sausages.

Socrates: No doubt that will soon be remedied by Charinus dear boy, but enough of this small talk, let's get down to the matter in hand. Ion, do you excel in reciting only Homer, or are you aware of a similar capability with regard to say, Hesiod or Archilochus?

Ion: No, I only possess this very great skill in regard to Homer, and I consider that this is sufficient to earn my livelihood.

Socrates: Tell me, are there any topics on which Homer and Hesiod say very much the same thing?

Ion: In my opinion, and I should know that, there are very many similarities.

Socrates: Do you demonstrate these similarities better in Homer or Hesiod?

Ion: Equally, in my opinion, Socrates.

Socrates: Very well. Now both Poets write about Divination do they not?

Ion: Yes, Socrates, they do.

Socrates: Do you think that you, or a Diviner, would make the best exposition, regarding the verses these Poets write about Divination?

Ion: Well Socrates, I have to admit rather reluctantly, that possibly a Diviner would, but I have my doubts.

Socrates: Let us suppose you were a Diviner, do you think you could explain their discrepancies on the subject of Divination, if you understand their agreements?

Ion: Obviously, of course I believe I could.

Socrates: Now how does it happen that you can express Homer and not Hesiod or other Poets in equal degree, as you previously admitted? Are Homer's subjects different for all the other Poets. Doesn't he mainly write about War, Society, the differences between brave heroes and cowards, the relationship between Mankind and the Gods, heaven, and hell. In general terms are not these the principal topics in Homer's poems?

Ion: Yes Socrates, as always, you hit the proverbial tent peg, neatly on the head.

Socrates: Thank you Ion. But other Poets surely compose verses on the same topics?

Ion: Yes, but none as well as Homer!

Socrates: Worse than Homer indeed?

Ion: Oh yes, much worse.

Socrates: So Homer is the best poet to write about such topics?

Ion: By Jupiter yes! Very much the best!

Socrates: Now consider this. Amongst a number of mathematicians trying to solve the same arithmetical problem, might not one person among them, clearly know who has given the correct answer?

Ion: Of course.

Socrates: Would it be the same person who had been aware of the wrong answer or another?

Ion: Obviously the same person.

Socrates: That is someone learned in Arithmetic?

Ion: Certainly.

Socrates: Good. Now let us consider food stuffs. Among a number of Dieticians giving opinions on the wholesomeness of different foods, would one person be able to judge the correctness of the opinions of those who judged rightly, and another on the incorrectness of others, or would the same person be capable to judge both?

Ion: The same again Socrates.

Socrates: What name would you give that person then?

Ion: An expert Dietician.

Socrates: Good. Then we may confidently assert then, that in all cases, that the same individual who is an expert, competent to judge the truth, may also judge the falsehood, of any assertion that is advanced on the same subject. Furthermore, he who is unqualified to judge the falsity of what is said on a given topic, is also incompetent to judge its truth.

Ion: Yes, that must be the case.

Socrates: So the same individual would either be competent or incompetent for both?

Ion: Yes!

Socrates: Did you not say that Homer, and the other poets, such as Hesiod and Archilochus, write on the same topics, but unequally. One better and the other worse.

Ion: Yes, I said that, and I speak the truth.

Socrates: So, if you are able to judge what is well composed by the one, you must also be able to judge what is ill composed by the other. Is that the case?

Ion: I believe it is.

Socrates: Then dear friend, we would not be making a mistake if we stated that the great Poet and Rhapsodist Ion, possesses a power of illustration regarding Homer and all other poets, especially as he affirms that the same person must be esteemed as a competent judge of all those who write on the same subjects; insomuch as those subjects are understood by him when spoken of by one poet, as the subject matter of almost all the poets is much the same.

Ion: [somewhat taken aback] Please tell me then, what can possibly be the reason, Socrates, that when any other poet apart from Homer is mentioned I cannot control my power of attention, and I feel utterly incapable of reciting anything worth while, and my mind seems to fall almost asleep? But when anyone makes even a mention of Homer, my mind applies itself effortlessly to the topic. I awaken as if from a trance, and a host of eloquent praises suggest themselves to my mind automatically?

Socrates: [almost patronisingly] It is not very difficult to find the answer to this dilemma, my dear boy. You see, you are evidently unable to declaim on Homer according to real Art or what we call real Knowledge. For if your art endowed you with this faculty, you would be equally capable of using it with regard to any other of the poets in the repertory. Surely Poetry as an art is entire and whole as a unit, not exclusive to one Poet only?

Ion: Yes, Socrates, I would more or less agree with that.

Socrates: Then the same consideration must be given to all the Arts, which are also severally one and entire. Are you brave enough to listen to what I understand about this, Ion?

Ion: Yes, by Jupiter. Socrates I am always delighted when I listen to a wise man expound, like your good self.

Socrates: It is you who are now approaching sagacity Ion, you who are a Rhapsodist, and therefore an actor and possibly a poet. But I am an unprofessional and private man, with no vested interest, so I am only able to speak the truth as I see it. Now see how worldly is the question I shall now pose. Is Painting an Art whole and entire?

Ion: Certainly, Socrates.

Socrates: Good! now pay attention dear boy. Did you ever know a person who was competent enough to judge the fine paintings of Polygnotus, Aglaophon's gifted son, and yet incompetent to judge the work of any other artist, on the supposition that the works of other painters, when being shown to him, he would be wholly at a loss and feel inclined to fall fast asleep, having lost all his faculty of reasoning on the pictures in question? But, whenever his opinion was required of say, the work of Polygnotus, he would wake up, pay full attention to the painting, and then discourse on it with powerful eloquence and keen perceptiveness?

Ion: No, I have never met such a person, by Zeus!

Socrates: Now did you ever know anyone skilled in determining the merits of the sculptures of say Daedalus, the brilliant son of Metion, or Epius, the talented son of Panopus, or the excellent Theodorus the Samian, or any other fine Sculptor, who was immediately at a loss, and felt sleepy the moment any time any other sculptor was mentioned?

Ion: No Socrates, I have never come across such a person.

Socrates: Ah! Neither do I think that you have ever met with a man professing himself to be an astute judge of fine Poetry and a great Rhapsodist into the bargain, and competent to criticise either the poems of Olympus, Thanyris, Orpheus, Phemius of Ithaca, then the same Rhapsodist, who the moment he came to see you, the Great Rhapsodist, Ion the Ephesian, would feel himself completely at a loss, sleepy, and utterly incompetent to judge whether you rhapsodised well or badly?

Ion: I am unable to refute you wise Socrates, you are to skilled a dialectician for me, but of this I am keenly aware. I excel all other Rhapsodists in the copiousness and beauty of my recitations of Homer, as all who have ever heard me will testify, and I win the first prize in all the many contests in which I compete. Yet in respect of other Poets I lose this skill. It is for you, my guide, philosopher, mentor and friend, to tell me what is the reason for this failure, if there be a plausible explanation, and how I could remedy such a failing?

Socrates: Settle down my dear Ion. Make yourself very comfortable on this couch over there. I am about to deliver a lengthy discourse on this matter in order to enlighten you on your plight.

I shall tell you, what appears to me to be the cause of your inequality of power in Rhapsodic performance. I regret that it is because you are not the true Master of Art and Knowledge for the real illustrative rendition of Homer as you pretend, but it is merely inspiration which moves you, such as that which resides in a magnet, and no more. For not only does a magnet possess the power of attracting iron rings, and it can communicate to them the power of attracting other iron rings, so that sometimes you may see a long chain of iron rings, and other metal substances, attached and suspended to one another by this mysterious, almost magical influence. As the power of the magnet circulates through all the links in the series, and attaches each to each, so the Muse, communicating through those whom she has first inspired, reaches all others capable of sharing in the same inspiration. The influence of that first enthusiasm, creates both a chain and a succession. [Socrates paused for breath, before developing his thesis further.]

For the authors of all those great poems whom we admire, do not attain to excellence through the rules of any art alone, but they compose their beautiful melodies of verse in a state of high exaltation, and as it were, are possessed by a spirit not of their own making. Thus the composers of lyrical poetry create their admired songs in a state of ecstacsy, like the Corybantes, who lose control over their reason in the enthusiasm of their sacred dance. During this supernatural possession they are excited by the rhythm and harmony which they communicate to men and women. Like the Bacchantes, who when possessed by the God, imagine they draw milk and honey from the streams, in which, when they come to their senses, they find nothing there but fresh water. For the souls of the poets, as poets tell us have a similar ministration for the world, that of inspiration.

They tell us that their souls fly like honey bees from flower to flower, and wandering over the herb gardens, blossoms, and lush green meadows with their ambrosial ever flowing fountains of the Muse, then return to us laden with the sweetness of melody and musicality. Thus armed with the rainbow plumes of vivid imagery, metaphor, allegory, simile, assonance, hyperbole, alliteration, prosody, metre, and rhyme they bring down some fragment of truth to our level of understanding and uplift our souls to theirs. For a truly good poet, as opposed to a mere versifier, is a being, ethereally light winged and sacred in his intent. He cannot compose any verse worth calling poetry until he becomes inspired, ecstatic and carried away by the topic and theme. So, those like your good self who recite varied , beautiful poems as for example those of Homer, are excellent in proportion to the extent of their participation in this divine influence of inspiration, and to the degree in which the Muse herself has descended. In short the best Poets are, and should be the interpreters of divine influences. They should not be like those who prostitute their skill by writing about plebeian or vulgar subjects, in a verse form which can hardly be distinguished from prose, lacking in musicality. Does this make sense to you Ion?

Ion: Yes, by Jupiter. My mind is enlightened by your words, Socrates, and it seems to me that the major poets all communicate with us in their poetry through divine inspiration and skill in poetics and prosody.

Socrates: Well put, Ion. And do you Rhapsodists interpret these poets successfully to us?

Ion: Yes, Socrates, indeed we do.

Socrates: So you interpret the interpreters, in fact?

Ion: Evidently.

Socrates: Now mark this well! Do not shrink from answering my question. When you recite well, and fill your audience with admiration; whether you sing of Ulysses storming the threshold of his palace, surprising the suitors, or pouring shafts of arrows at his feet; or of brave Achilles assailing bold Hector; or those emotional passages concerning Andromache, Hecuba or Priam; are you then in possession of your Self or not? Or rather, are you not rapt and filled with such enthusiasm by the deeds that you declaim, that you merely fancy you are in Ithica or Troy, or wherever the Epic takes you?

Ion: You are most accurate in your analysis Socrates. I cannot honestly deny it; for when I recite of sorrow, my eyes are filled with tears. And when I speak of fearful and terrible deeds, I suffer from horripilation, my hair stands up on end, my flesh breaks out in goose pimples, and my heart starts to beat rapidly.

Socrates: Tell me then Ion. Can we call him to be really firm in himself, in control of his mind and senses, who weeps while dressed in luxurious robes, crowned with a golden coronal, and while not losing any of these paraphernalia is filled with fear when surrounded by ten thousand friendly persons, not one of whom desires to cause him any harm?

Ion: To be truthful Socrates, I could not.

Socrates: Do you often see your audience to be moved in a similar vein as your good self?

Ion: Yes, very many among them, and often. When I stand on my rostrum, and I see them weeping, with their eyes fixed, staring at me, completely overcome by my recitation, I reflect that really I have no grreat need to agitate them in this way. For if they weep, inwardly I laugh, taking their money. If they should laugh ironically, then I must inwardly weep, going without their hard earned cash.

Socrates: I didn't know you were a Cynic Ion as well as a Rhapsodist. But do you now perceive that your audience is the final link in that chain which I have described as held together by the power of the magnet? You Thespians and Rhapsodists are the middle links of which the Poet is the first, and through all these, the Muse influences whichever mind he chooses, as they conduct this power the one to the other. And so, like iron rings strung together by the magnet, so hang a long series of choruses, dancers, teachers, poets, critics, pedagogues, and audiences all attracted by the Muse.

Some poets are influenced by one Muse, some by another; we call them possessed, and this term really expresses the truth, for they are held by them. You Ion are possessed by the Muse of Homer. If you recite the works of lesser poets, you immediately become drowsy, and forget your lines. But with Homer, you become excessively excited and grow eloquent. For all that you declaim from Homer is derived from divine inspiration. This answers your question, that you excel from inspiration rather than the Knowledge and Art of what constitutes good poetry.

Ion: You speak well Socrates. Yet I am somewhat surprised and perplexed that you describe me as almost insane and possessed when I recite Homer. Also I believe I have real Art and Knowledge of Homer and all that constitutes the best Poetry. I do not think I shall appear, as a mad man to you like this, when you come to hear me.

Socrates: I wish to hear you one day. But not before you have answered one important question. What topic does Homer treat best? Surely he does not treat all subjects equally?

Ion: I suppose you must be aware that he treats of almost everything.

Socrates: Does Homer ever mention topics on which you are an ignoramus?

Ion: No, what can those possibly be?

Socrates: Does not Homer write on skills such as chariot driving, for example? If I can recall his verses, I will quote them.

Ion: Do not try Socrates, I remember them well.

Socrates: Repeat for me then what Nestor says to his son Antilochus, counselling him to be cautious in turning, during the chariot race at the funeral games of Patroclus.

Ion: [recites]
"For your self, lean slightly in one's golden car, of course
To the left of them;
then call upon your faithful horse with whip and voice,
and by hand give him good free rein.
And at the final post let the near horse come quite near,
So the nave of your well-wrought wheel shall appear
To graze the stone. But beware less that stone you strike!"
[while reciting Ion is trance-like gripping and pulling at imaginary reins to the left and right]
That is from the Iliad Chapter 23 line 335 I believe, Socrates.

Socrates: Enough. Now tell me Ion, would a physician or a charioteer be the better judge as to Homer's knowledge on this subject?

Ion: Obviously the charioteer.

Socrates: Because he understands that skill- or for some other reason?

Ion: Obviously again, from his knowledge of the skill of chariot driving rather than medicine.

Socrates: So we see that one science is unable to judge another. A good steersman, for example, does not understand Hippocrates or medicine?

Ion: You are stating the obvious again, Socrates, yes, without a doubt.

Socrates: No is a physician able to understand architecture?

Ion: Obviously not Socrates! What are you driving at? like a charioteer yourself by these obvious questions?

Socrates: Well said, Ion [smiling]. Is it not so with every art, craft, science and skill? If we become adept in one, we're often ignorant in another. But first, tell me, do not all these arts differ one from the other?

Ion: Yes, they do, considerably.

Socrates: So we can say with certainty, rather than from opinion, that when we say an Art is the Knowledge of one thing, we do not mean that it is the Knowledge of another.

Ion: Certainly, Socrates, that is clear.

Socrates: [with some animation] Then, if each art contained the Knowledge of all things and the Gods forbid that should ever happen, and even that baffling knowledge of the Thing in Itself! Why should we give them different names? Surely we do so that we may distinguish one field of knowledge from another. As you well know there are five fingers on each hand [holding up his palm], and if I asked you whether we both meant the same thing or something else, when we speak of counting in arithmetic- would you not say the 'same thing'?

Ion: Yes, of course, Socrates [beads of perspiration were beginning to break out on Ion's face]. Why do you keep on repeating the obvious?

Socrates: You will understand why, in due course. Now wipe your brow you are sweating. Would you like some water?

Ion: No, it is all right Socrates, let us continue. I am keen to see you get to the point.

Socrates: Now tell me, when we learn one Art we must learn everything with regard to it its application in order to excel, and entirely other things if we learn another?

Ion: Indeed, Socrates [wearily].

Socrates: And he who is not very well versed in that particular Art cannot be a good judge or critic of what is said or done in it?

Ion: True, Socrates, but go on.... please.

Socrates: To return to the verses which you so animatedly recited, do you think you, or a charioteer, would be more capable in deciding whether Homer had spoken accurately or inaccurately in that matter?

Ion: I think the charioteer would, Socrates.

Socrates: Good. For you are a very capable Rhapsodist but a hopeless charioteer aren't you dear boy? [somewhat sardonically]

Ion: Yes, that is so. I have sadly neglected that most useful skill.

Socrates: Now when Homer introduces Hecamede the best and most beautiful of all Nestor's delightful, I nearly said rhapsodic, concubines, giving Machaeon a much needed medicinal potion to drink, he says

"She grated goat's milk cheese into finest Pramnian wine,

With a brazen grater, adding onion as a relish just in time."

That is from the Iliad Chapter II:Line 639-40, if I am not mistaken.

Ion: Yes, Socrates, you are right. I admire your memory.

Socrates: Good. Does that quotation belong to the medical or rhapsodical art, to decide whether or not Homer speaks correctly on the subject.

Ion: The medical, of course, what kind of a fool do you think I am, Socrates?

Socrates: Calm down please dear boy, I am trying to teach and help you. Now when he says-

"She dived to the bottom like a leaden singing box,

Which mounted on the horny tip of a strong field ox

Speeds it's way, bringing trouble to ever hungry fish."

That is also from the Iliad Chapter 24. Line 80, if I am not mistaken?

Ion: Right again, Socrates.

Socrates: Does it belong to the Piscatorial or the Rhapsodic art to decide whether he writes correctly or not?

Ion: The art of fishing, obviously, Socrates.

Socrates: Now consider carefully whether you are not moved to make some such request as this to me:- 'Come on, Socrates, since you have been shrewd enough to have discovered in Homer's vast work an accurate description of all these arts and skills, help me in my inquiry as to his competence on the subject of soothsayers and divination. For he often treats of them in the Odyssey, especially when he introduces Theoclymenus the Soothsayer of the Melampians, prophesying to the Suitors declaiming thus -

[Socrates reached for a nearby stool pretending it was a rostrum, and mounted as if to recite, burlesquing the manner of a Rhapsodist.] Plato seemed rather shocked at this irreverence and put down his scribbling block. Ion flushed angrily, as if poised to stamp out in a huff, but somehow controlled himself and stayed put. [Socrates obviously enjoying the humour of the moment waves his arms in the air and declaims]

"Are your shaven heads, your shrunken faces and your limbs below,

All kindled with the sound of weeping while your cheeks are wet with woe,

While the porch is filled with ghosts and the hall is filled with some,

Rushing hellwards, beneath the gloom of a blood red setting

Sun;

It has perished out of heaven, and a wicked mist engulfs the worlds."

That is from the Odyssey Chapter 20. Lines351-5 if I am not mistaken.

Ion: Right again Socrates. You should have been a Rhapsodist rather than a Philosopher. [We all laughed at Socrates' banal parody, except for Ion who looked somewhat put out and then coldly said...]

Ion: Your mimicry was very funny Socrates, ha! Ha! but hardly an accurate rendition of the sacred text. Your childish sense of satire distorted your memory, now what is your point?

Socrates: [ignored him and said] Calm down Ion, that is no way to speak to your Master, and I haven't finished yet. Homer also says in the Iliad, at the Battle of the Walls,

[Again he waves his arms and declaims loudly in a sonorous voice]

"As they were keen to cross, a huge bird, sped straight overhead;

An eagle on high, it skirted round the host sighted on its left;

In its claws it held a huge blood red snake, oh so very, very deft!

Struggling, the snake did not forget the joy of battle's quest.

Writhing on its self, it struck the bird that held it on its breast

Behind its throat; at this blow it let the snake fall swiftly down,

In the painful agony of death, right far away and very far along,

It dropped straight into the middle of the multitudinous throng.

With a lusty screech the eagle flew away, on the gusty wind's fair crown."

That was from the Iliad, Chapter 12 Lines 200-9 was it not?

[Socrates then stepped down from the stool to the laughter

and amusement of us all, except for Ion, bowing as for applause.]

Ion: I apologise Socrates, you are indeed a great wit.

Socrates: I hereby assert Ion, that it belongs to a true Soothsayer both to observe and to judge such appearances as these.

Ion: [having recovered his calm] Yes, Socrates I quite agree with you. Well done, now what of it?

Socrates: So you see I have recited some passages relating to soothsaying, medicine and fishing, and as you are more learned than I, please tell me whatever relates here to the Rhapsodist and his Art. For a Rhapsodist is competent above all others to consider and pronounce on such matters.

Ion: And with great respect Socrates, and to everything else mentioned by Homer!

Socrates: Do not be forgetful, Ion.

Ion: And what do I forget?

Socrates: Don't you recall that you admitted that the skill of reciting verses was somewhat different from that of driving chariots?

Ion: Yes, I do remember.

Socrates: And furthermore, did you not admit that in so far as they are different, that the subjects included in their knowledge must also be different?

Ion: Certainly, I did.

Socrates: So now you will never assert again that the art of the Rhapsodist is that of Universal Knowledge. Even a Rhapsodist, as perfect and sublime as you, may be ignorant on many things.

Ion: Except, perhaps, such subjects as we now discuss, Socrates.

Socrates: What do you mean by 'such subjects', besides those which relate to the other arts? And which among them do you profess to have a competent acquaintance with, since not with all?

Ion: [becoming heated] I venture to think that the good

Rhapsodist has a perfect knowledge of what is becoming for any man to speak; and for any woman, any slave, any free man, any ruler, any citizen and so on.

Socrates: Calm down dear boy. But how do you think that a Rhapsodist knows better than the Pilot, what the Captain of a ship, caught in a tempest ought to say?

Ion: In that particular case, I grant that the Pilot would know best.

Socrates: Has the Rhapsodist or the Physician the clearest knowledge of what should be said to an invalid?

Ion: The Physician [sulkingly]

Aeschines: [Thinking to himself. I pity poor Ion, when we reach this point in any Dialogue, I feel that Socrates is like the cat that plays with the mouse before he kills him.]

Socrates: But you insist that he knows what a slave should say?

Ion: Of course.

Socrates: Let's take as an example, the driving of cattle. A Rhapsodist, in your opinion, would know much better than the Herdsman what should be said to a slave engaged in bringing back a herd of wild oxen.

Ion: No, not in that instance.

Socrates: How about what a woman should say about spinning wool, compared to a weaver?

Ion: Of course not, Socrates. How can you ask such foolish questions?

Socrates: Come, come, my dear boy, patience.... I am getting to the salient point. Now, would a Rhapsodist know what a man, who is a General, should say when exhorting his troops to go into battle?

Ion: Yes! A Rhapsodist would certainly know that.

Socrates: Oh really? Are Poetic Recitations and Battle Strategies the same skills?

Ion: I know what is appropriate for a General to say at that moment.

Socrates: Oh? Probably because you are experienced in the art of warfare? Imagine if you are equally expert in horsemanship and playing the harp, you would obviously know whether a man rode well or badly. But I am trying to get you to admit, who understands riding best? the horseman or the harpist? Well?

Ion: Obviously the horseman [showing some irritation].

Socrates: And if you knew a good harpist, you would say in the same way that he or she would better understand what is a good harp performance better than a horseman?

Ion: Obviously.

Socrates: Since you understand battle strategy so well, perhaps you can tell me which is the best, the art of warfare or rhapsody?

Ion: One does not seem to me to be better or worse than the other.

Socrates: Oh, one is not better than the other? Would you say that battle tactics and poetic performance are two separate skills or one?

Ion: They appear to me to be the same skill.

Socrates: So, a good Rhapsodist is also a good General?

Ion: Of course, he could be.

Socrates: And a good General is also a good Rhapsodist?

Ion: I do not claim that to be the case.

Socrates: You said that a good Rhapsodist was also a good General.

Ion: Yes, I did.

Socrates: Are you not the best Rhapsodist in Greece?

Ion: By far, Socrates, in my opinion and in the world's estimation.

Socrates: And you are also the most excellent Commander in Warfare among the Greeks?

Ion: Yes, I am. I learned that art from Homer.

Socrates: How is it then Ion, by Zeus, that being both the finest General and the best Rhapsodist among us, you continually wander about Greece rhapsodising, and never lead the Greek Army on to glorious victory?! Does it seem to you that Greece badly needs Gold Crowned Rhapsodists, and has no need of brilliant Generals?

Ion: My native town Socrates is ruled by yours. She requires no General for her wars. And what is more, neither your city nor the Lacedemonians will elect me to lead their armies- they both think that their own Generals are quite adequate.

Socrates: My good Ion, are you familiar with Apollodorus the Cyzicenian?

Ion: What do you mean by that?

Socrates: Well, he it was, that though a stranger, the Athenians often elected him to be their General. What is more, Phanosthenes the Andrian, and Heraclides the Clazomenian were both foreigners, but this City has chosen them, being great men, to lead its armies and fill other high offices. Should not therefore, you, the great Ion the Ephesian, be elected and honoured if he was thought to be so capable in the heroic Art of Warfare? [Socrates smirking]. Were not the gallant and courageous Ephesians originally from Athens. But if you spoke truly Ion, and praise Homer according to the principles of Art and Knowledge, well, you have certainly grossly deceived me, and have disappointed me greatly! You will not explain in which sphere you are remarkably clever, but like Proteus, you change from one thing to another, and to escape at last you disappear in the form of a great General. If therefore you possess the learning which you promised to expound on the subject of Homer, you have failed miserably! But if you were really honest and declared that your eloquence in reciting Homer is only from Inspiration and not through Knowledge then I would be able to forgive you.

Ion: [humbly] Yes, Socrates, you win. I am humbled. It is far better for me to be regarded as Inspired and not as a learned and knowledgeable Eulogist of Homer.

Socrates: Well said, dear boy. Let us now adjourn for some light refreshments after that battle. Aeschines, what a pity you didn't bring some of your wonderful sausages! Have some more wine.

Chapter 5

Psyche or a Dream Within a Dream

This is a completely unknown and newly discovered Dialogue of Socrates that Aeschines recorded. It seems Plato was not invited to Socrates' House for this select Symposium or we would have his inherited his record. I believe this previously unknown Dialogue to be of very great importance and an important contribution to our understanding of Socratic Philosophy. It demonstrates his debt to Far-Eastern thought. We are indeed fortunate that Aeschines was invited, and that I was able to make the discovery. It is my favourite translation of the works I have discovered. I am greatly privileged to be able to reveal it to the world after well over two millenia. - *E.R.S.*

Present: Socrates, Alciabides, Antisthenes, Hermogenes, Critobulus, Autolicus, Hermogenes, Niceratus and Aeschines

Socrates: I have called you all together, those of you whom I regard as my more mature disciples, although all of you still need much more roasting in my fire, a great deal more, if I may say so. To this effect, this evening I wish to present you all with an allegory.

Alciabedes: [interrupting] You mean something like the allegory you told us about once before. The 'Cave' I think it was called. Plato read it to us from his record of the Dialogue you once gave on an Ideal State, The Republic, I think he named it.

Socrates: Yes, it's something like that except this allegory is not concocted, it is about a dream that actually happened to me, and is as real as we are now, relatively speaking, as you will no doubt see.

Niceratus: Yes, Homer had a great deal to say about dreams, shall I recite some verses?

Socrates: No! Niceratus Hold your peace. Please do not interrupt me again, you, or any of you, or I will send you all packing!

Niceratus: I am sorry Socrates.

Socrates: To continue after that rudeness. Last night I had an uncannily vivid dream. I dreamed I was delivering a discourse on Politics to those of you I have invited here this evening, in this house, and this is what happened. In the middle of the dream, it was as if I had woken up, and was fully conscious, although I was actually still dreaming. I suddenly stopped my discourse, and said rather abruptly to all of you in my dream "Do you all realise that I am addressing dream figures, you are all dream figures in my dream, none of you are actually real!" Then it was you Antisthenes who spoke."Nonsense!" you said, " Socrates! We are as real as you are at this moment and this is definitely not a dream?" Then there was a hubbub and many of you echoed Antisthenes, and said words to the effect " No, Socrates, you are wrong, we are all as awake as you are!" At that moment I woke up and there I was in bed with Xantippe who was snoring beside me, so I knew it must have been a dream. The strange thing was that I felt I was actually fully conscious and aware, like I am now, in this dream. How do you explain it? Speak up, please.

[Socrates paused to see the effect. There was stony silence, then he spoke some more.]

Socrates: Please speak now , if you wish, any of you, ask questions, say what you like, except for reciting Homer.

[There was again silence, then Hermogenes eventually spoke up.]

Hermogenes: It is most strange Socrates that a man can wake up in the middle of a dream, but still be in the dream, but I suppose it is possible. Once I was dreaming about Alciabiades here, I won't tell you in what connection, it was rather intimate....

Alciabiades: [blushed] Oh, I say... please tell me sometime when we are alone. It sounds most intriguing. Please continue dear.

Hermogenes: Then in the middle of this encounter, I suddenly felt that I was actually dreaming, that it was all really a dream, and I woke up, rather disappointed not to have finished my somewhat delightful reverie.

Socrates: Yes, Hermogenes. It is something like that, but my dream went on much longer when I felt I was awake, and it was a much stronger feeling. It had the taste of full awareness. I truly knew I was awake in my dream, and you were all dream figures created by my brain, I suppose.

Critobulus: It seems unbelievable Socrates, but I believe you, you always tell us the truth [the others nodded in affirmation].

Socrates: Good. Well I will tell you what this dream means to me. There is no doubt it was a message from my own Self, the core of my own Being, my innermost, the Divine spark wit in me, you could say. We all have an atom, a Microcosm of the Divine Macrocosm inside our hearts. The problem is that it is obscured by all the rubbish we have accumulated in this life and previous lives. It forms a veil over the Real Self, and we live in a state of ignorance. The only way to remove this veil is through self scrutiny, investigation and enquiry along with devotion to the One Good or God, if you prefer.

So this dream came from that Self, I am certain about it. It was unmistakably of a different quality to other dreams. Most of them I forget immediately, but this one I will never, ever forget. What it says to me that it was an allegory, a metaphor if you like, that we are all in the dream of life, now, at this very moment. You think you are all awake , but I am the only awakened one among you, that is why you love and respect me as your Teacher.

Aeschines: [I could not contain myself from speaking] Do you mean to say Socrates, that we are dream figures in a dream now at this moment?!. How is such a thing possible?

Socrates: Well dear sausage maker, yes. We are all dream figures in a dream discussing how to wake up, from time to time.

Aeschines: I am afraid I don't understand. The world seems so real and the dream a fantasy.

Socrates: Never fear Aschines, you think you are the body, but that is only a form which appears in the dream of life. Behind each bodily form lies the formless 'I AM' your pure conscious sense of your real existence. Your very being, in fact.

Aeschines: But Socrates.....

Socrates: Here we go again the eternal But... tell me what is your But this time?

Aeschines: But Socrates, this world answers to my all my senses, I touch things and they feel as if they are truly there and real.

Socrates: These senses are very great deceivers dear boy. Heraclitus told us long ago that everything was made of atoms, in a state of flux. What you touched a moment ago is not the same object as that which you touch again, now. It only seems so. Yes, seems is a good word, everything seems to be real, but is an illusory world which I liken to a fantastic dream, and you are all dream figures talking about waking up from this dream, now at this very moment. This mind that creates our dream of life, and dreams so well, is the same mind that dreams in our sleep.

Antisthenes: Socrates this is very far fetched, to say the least. In our dreams at night, when we wake up there are no consequences. In my dream last night, I dreamed I was run over by a chariot driven by you of all people Socrates. When I woke up, I was safe and uninjured, I knew it was a dream.

Socrates: Well, Antisthenes, I cannot drive a chariot like young Autolicus here. Some dreams do have consequences. They can be clairvoyant, and linger on to affect your waking state, but be that as it may. The point is that just as night dreams draw their material from the waking state, the dream of life draws its material from habits formed in previous lives, and new habits formed in this life. When we die, all our habits are carried by the immortal Soul into its next life which the Gods choose for us, in order to assist our spiritual development. Everything is preordained, We act from necessity, not free will, as I have often told you. This world is unreal, as I have often said. The real world is beyond this dream, and you shall know it when you wake up. To awaken you is my job, and its very difficult with such numbskulls.

Critobalus: I am far from convinced Socrates. It goes against everyman's experience and common sense.

Socrates: Your so called common sense is vulgar ignorance dear boy. But to be serious for a moment. Yes, man is asleep, but mankind imagines they are awake in the real sense. Let me explain further. But before doing so let us have some wine mingled with fresh water. Alciabides fetch the flasks. [Alciabides leaves, then returns with a tray of flasks each containing wine and water.] Now you are all refreshed I will continue. Please pay attention and stop your perverted minds from flitting about so much, like mischievous monkeys, from thought to thought, all the time. Here is a verse I composed this morning.

"The World, seen by the poor soul,

Lapsed from its own true Being,

Buried in darkness, now believing

That it is only the body so whole.

The world thus seen is not existing."

Alciabides: Not up to your usual standard Socrates.

Socrates: [ignores the interruption] I shall now explain. In the stage that you are in of being spiritual aspirants, like all of you here, I must tell you that the world is like a dream, an illusion. There is no other way. When a man forgets he is God, who is Real, permanent and omnipresent, and deludes himself into thinking that he is a mere body in the universe which is filled with other bodies, that are also transitory, and labours under that delusion,

I have to remind him that the world is unreal, like a dream and a delusion. Why? Because his vision which has forgotten its own Self is dwelling in the external material universe. It will not turn inwards into Self examination unless I impress on him that all of this external universe is unreal. How many times have I told you that the unexamined life is not worth living! When once he or she realises his own Self, and also knows that there is nothing other than his own Self, he will come to look upon the whole universe as God. Like very many of you, at first I found it very difficult to be convinced that the world we perceive is 'unreal'. I realised through reasoning that the concepts of space, time, and causality are inherent in my organ of cognition, the brain if you like, and the Self creates the screen of consciousness on which the world stage, actions and pictures are projected. Also as I have already confirmed that what we see, feel, smell , touch and taste is not what it appears to be, but subtle energies in constant movement or in a state of flux. In truth I shall give you some maxims.

1. All is Absolute, pure, infinite Consciousness, non-dual, Supreme Intelligence, the Self-Existent Self or God

2.. The powers of veiling and projection are inherent powers in the Godhead.

3. These powers manifest an apparent, but unreal Universe. Unreal because it was Not before manifestation and will Not Be after dissolution.

Therefore it is likened to a dream in the Supreme Intelligence or Mind of the Godhead. Thus the apparent Universe is but an appearance superimposed on the same Godhead. It does not exist apart from 'That'. It could be termed, therefore, a confusion between the Real and the Unreal, or neither Real nor Unreal, or both Real and Unreal. The definition of the term Real is applied to the Immutable or Unchanging. The apparent world is constantly changing, in a state of flux, becoming and decaying, so it cannot be termed Real in this sense, whereas the Godhead is immutable, unchanging and eternal, and thus may be termed

Real.

4. The ignorant individual soul is reborn and dies continuously through many lifetimes, until he or she learns to know its own dear Self. It carries forward in each new life time, the seeds of many latent tendencies from previous lives. Athough its True Nature is also the Absolute Pure Consciousness of the Godhead, but because of the implicit projection and veiling, inherent in the Self of Pure Consciousness it identifies with its insentient body and creates a Universe from its latent tendencies and habits through the mind, our organ of cognition, the brain and its sensorial adjuncts. The mind is a wondrous power in the Self. The world it sees, composed of latent tendencies , and thoughts is therefore of the nature of a dream, even an hallucination, and may be termed 'unreal'.

5. The latent tendencies inherent in each Soul at the time of each new life, are selected by the Gods, who are merely adjuncts of the Supreme Godhead, for his or her spiritual development. So all is benign, based on Love, essentially.

6. The mind-body complex, personal individuality, other sentient beings, and the Universe of multiplicity, are all therefore a superimposition on the Self which is now living from reflected Consciousness, mirrored by egotism and the latent tendencies.

7. Through Grace, the Soul receives the teachings of Self Knowledge from somebody like myself, and when fit, through assimilation of this Knowledge and mental purification through right intellectual discrimination, spiritual practice and devotion, he or she is shown the way to awaken from this dream of suffering and transient joy .

The means are through investigation into the source of the ego, the Self and the illusory nature of the Universe.

8. At the same time one lives one life as if it was real, knowing it to be unreal, and accepting all that happens as ultimately for the best.

9. When there is an awakening from the dream of life, the

transmigration of the Soul is over for good. The immortal Self of infinite Consciousness is Realised directly and one lives from that state until the mind-body falls off in death.

Then one is absorbed into the Godhead or Infinite Consciousness, no longer a separate individual identified with its body-mind. All is the Self, and the world is seen to be Real because its substratum is now known to be the Godhead.

Alciabides: That was very profound Socrates. You have explained a great deal, and we have very much to ponder on. I trust Aeschines, who has been taking notes, will pass on his scribblings to us so we can consider the matter in depth and then question you at another time.

Socrates: Yes, Alciabides that is a very sensible suggestion. We will adjourn until Aeschines writes up his record which I shall confirm. Copies will be made for each of you, and we shall meet again.

So now let us let go. Drink our wine and Niceratus, will kindly entertain us with some Homer, and Aeschines, I see you have brought some sausages with you for us to enjoy. [I ceased recording, and we all enjoyed ourselves, quite forgetting we were only dream figures living in a dream.]

Chapter 6

The Admonishment of His Son

[This Dialogue is not recorded by Plato, but briefly reported by Xenophon who must have heard it from Aeschines. - *E.R.S.*]

One day Socrates heard that Lamprocles his eldest son had been very angry with his mother Xantippe, and so Socrates wished to talk with him. I was calling on Socrates that day to deliver my notes on his recent Dialogues for him to scrutinise and hopefully approve. When Lamprocles arrived, Socrates asked me to remain, as we still had more work to do together. Thus I was privileged to hear this remarkable admonishment of his eldest son.

Socrates: Tell me my son, have you ever heard that certain persons are called 'The Ungrateful'?

Lamprocles: Certainly, Father.

Socrates: And do you know how these men behave who are given this title?

Lamprocles: I do indeed. For they are men or women who receive some kindness, and do not reciprocate when they can. These other men call 'The Ungrateful'.

Socrates: That is correct, so, do they then appear to you to class the ungrateful with the unjust?

Lamprocles: Yes, that is possibly the case.

Socrates: And do you understand the way in which these people act that they call these people ungrateful and unjust?

Lamprocles: I do. For those that have benefited from some kindness, and do not return it with an act of kindness on their part, other men call them ungrateful and think them to be unjust.

Socrates: And have you ever considered, the paradox, why it is thought to be unjust to make slaves of our friends, but it is just to make slaves of our enemies; and unjust to be ungrateful to our friends, and just to be ungrateful towards our enemies?

Lamprocles: I have gone into that question Socrates, and consider that from whomever a man receives a favour, whether friend or enemy, and does not try to reciprocate the favour could be considered, in my opinion, unjust.

Socrates: If that is the case then ingratitude must be manifest injustice, do you agree?

Lamprocles: Yes, Father.

Socrates: So the greater the benefits a man or woman receives and makes no return, the more unjust he or she must be?

Lamprocles: Yes, that follows. [Little does Lamprocles suspect that he is like a mouse sniffing the cheese on a mouse trap - one bite and then bang!]

Socrates: Whom than can you conceive receiving greater benefits from any person than children receive from their parents? Little babies whom their mothers and fathers have brought up from non existence to existence, to see so much beauty around them, to share in so many blessings, as the gods grant to mankind. Your dear, conscientious mother nursed you with sweet milk from her own bountiful breast at birth. Every good thing a young boy required to see him through this troubled vale of tears was heaped upon you. You were encouraged, corrected, housed, fed, clothed, educated and supplied with all that loving parents could possibly bestow upon you. Every blessing which is beyond human valuation, such as love and support were heaped upon you, my dear boy. You do not surely suppose that men and women beget children merely to gratify their passions since the streets, brothels and public baths, offer many different means to allay such common desires. As parents we prayed that the finest children may be born to us, to be able to rear them as good citizens and turn out to be truly virtuous men and women. So we came together, not from lust, but with a higher purpose. When men of wisdom choose a wife they look for one who will be a good mother and be capable of bearing and rearing good children. So we marry and unite with them with that end in view. When she gives birth to a child, she bears great pain, and then suckles the new born babe and cherishes it with all her heart, soul and mind. She tries to satisfy all its calls and needs, not knowing what benefit she will ever receive from the new born babe. As soon as the child is capable of learning she teaches it with love and affection. She will do everything in her power to protect the child from sickness, and if, the gods forbid, he or she becomes ill, she will nurse him or her, back to robust health.

[Lamprocles remains silent somewhat abashed]

Well, son speak up!

[Lamprocles stayed silent for a little longer, and then spoke]

Lamprocles: Well father you are wise, but there is another side to all this which you fail to take into account. Even if she has done everything you say, and even more than that, no one assuredly could endure the difficult times when she is in ill-humour?

Socrates: What, Lamprocles is harder to endure, the fury of a wild beast or that of a mother?

Lamprocles: I regret to say, often a mother, such as mine.

Socrates: Oh! Has she ever inflicted any hurt upon you, by biting, kicking, mauling, like many suffer from wild beasts?

Lamprocles: No, Socrates. But, by Jupiter, she says such things that nobody would endure to hear, not even for the value of all that she owns.

Socrates: And have you considered, my boy, how much grievous trouble and distress you have given her by your peevishness, your utterances, your actions, by day and night, and how much anxiety you have caused her by your sulkiness and bad moods?

Lamprocles: I deny that Socrates. I have never said or done anything to her at which she or I could feel ashamed.

Socrates: Look here Lamprocles. Do you think then it is more difficult for you to listen to what she says to admonish you, than for actors to bear, when they utter the bitterest reproaches against one another in the Stage Tragedies?

Lamprocles: Oh, actors endure such verbal attacks easily, because they know them to be feigned; and that the actor who utters such abuse does not really intend any real harm.

Socates: Yet, you are displeased with your mother, although in your heart, you know that whatever she says to you is only with the intent of doing good to you, and improving your character and behaviour. Or do you falsely imagine that your mother actually wishes you harm?

Lamprocles: No, Socrates, I do not think that for one moment she wishes me harm.

Socrates: [displaying signs of anger] Do you really think that your mother who has been so good towards you, who is ever watchful, anxious to take care of you in sickness and in health to the utmost of her powers, and prays to the gods that every blessing may pour upon your head, can be called a harsh mother? I am quickly coming to the conclusion, my boy, that if you cannot endure your mother, than you cannot endure anything that is good for you at all. Tell me, whether in principle, you think you should pay respect to any other human being, or are you determined to pay respect to nobody, not even to the orders of an Army General or a Naval Commander?

Lamprocles: No, Socrates, absolutely not, I have never formed any such resolution!

Socrates: Are you then agreeable to cultivating your neighbours' good will, so that they may be willing help you when you need aid in case you meet with a domestic misfortune at home and need assistance?

Lamprocles: Yes, I am.

Socrates: Or would it make no difference whatsoever if a fellow traveller on a journey or any other person you met on your trip was a friend or an enemy? Or would you cultivate their good will?

Lamprocles: [reflecting a moment] Yes, Socrates, I think I would.

Socrates: Oh! So you are prepared to pay attention and respect to such persons, don't you think, therefore, that you should pay equal, if not more respect to your own fond mother, who happens to love you more than anyone else in the whole world? Are you aware that legally, the State rules, that if a man fails to respect his own parents then he will never be allowed to hold an Archonship! [One of nine chief magistrates in the State of Athens - *E.R.S.*]

Also if a son or daughter fails to maintain the sepulchres of their dead parents, the State will institute an enquiry into the cause, in the examinations of candidates for Office. So, my son, if you are wise, you will pray to the gods to pardon you for lacking the necessary respect for your mother, unless everyone look upon you as an ungrateful person, and withhold any benefits that may flow from their hands. For if men and women reach the conclusion that you are ungrateful to your loving parents, no one will believe that if he or she does you a good turn that they will meet with any gratitude in return! How about that?

Lamprocles: You are right, father, I repent, and confess my failings. I will find mother immediately and ask for her forgiveness.

Socrates: Good, Lamprocles. Now we must not keep patient Aeschines waiting any longer, we have work to do, so lets all share a glass of wine and a sausage together, and call it a day.

Chapter 7

My Memories of Socrates

This is the last, but one, of the documents found in the Aschines' Phial that Dr. Sekers discovered in Cairo. It is not a Dialogue but a series of reminiscences penned by the ubiquitous sausage maker.

1. On the Value of Friendship

[These recollections are not found in the works of Plato. - E.R.S.]

It is my sincere wish to leave a record of some of my memories concerning my beloved Master, and leave for posterity some accounts, that I recall, to illustrate the wisdom and magnanimity of this exceptionally noble man who was one of the leading citizens of Athens.

I heard him on one auspicious occasion, holding a discourse concerning Friends, when he said that a true and honest friend was one of the most valuable possessions that a man or woman could possibly have. Yet in spite of that he observed that the majority of mankind were attending to anything rather than securing good friends. He noticed that they were industriously hell bent on acquiring new houses, land, slaves, cattle, furniture and gold. As for friends, they seemed ignorant about how to make them and what is more how to keep them. He saw that even when their slaves were sick they called in Physicians, but paid little or no attention to their so called friends. If both died, they grieved for the loss of the slave which they felt they had personally suffered, but considered that they lost little or nothing on losing a friend. Of their many possessions they exercised the utmost vigilance, but neglected their friends when they needed care and attention. Not even, that, but when asked how many true friends they really have, they have great diffi-culty in remembering how many, if at all. It amazes me, because in comparison with all their other possessions what could be better than a trusted friend whom one loves, and will exert every effort to aid one in times of need?

2. The Art of the Military Commander

Socrates often gave advice to his friends and acquaintances on performing their public duties well. Here are three such incidents I recall. It all went to show how patriotic Socrates was, in always encouraging and advising those whom he met, how to benefit the State, and not as his wicked detractors tried to make out, that he was only interested in corrupting the youth of Athens. But more of that scandal and what followed later in my final chapter.

Once he heard that Dionysodorus had arrived in Athens, offering to teach the art of General-ship to the young men aspiring to become army commanders. I was with Socrates when he was talking to a youth who greatly wished to become a high ranking military officer. This is what I remember him saying. "It is unbecoming, young man, that anyone who aspires to be a commander of an army in this country, should ever neglect learning the duties of that office when he has a good opportunity of learning them." So he induced the young man to go and see Dionysodaurus who had a reputation as a teacher of Warfare. Some time later, the same youth met up with Socrates again, while I was with him, and the conversation ran like this. Socrates playfully said to those of us with him, "Since Homer has repre-sented that great General Agamemnon as highly dignified, does not this young man, after being instructed in the art of Generalship, seem to be much more dignified than before? Let him tell us what he learned from the worthy Dionysodorus." The youth replied, "He began with the same thing with which he finished - tactics and not much else." "Oh", said Socrates, looking somewhat surprised, and said, "how very small a part of the qualifications of a good General is that? For a successful General must be capable of teaching all that is needed for warfare, especially in securing provisions for his troops, otherwise they will become starved and disgruntled, and their morale will be defeatist. A good General must be a man of great ingenuity, careful in planning every move, persevering, sagacious, kind, and yet severe. He must plan that he has the necessary overwhelming force which will assure victory. He must be open in his demeanour, yet cunning: careful of his own men, but ready to take men from other Generals, less capable than he is himself. He must be eager and skilled to acquire wealth in order to finance the Army. He must be cautious, yet enterprising, and above all, very brave in every circumstance, come what may. Of course it is important to be skilled in tactics as well, for a well arranged army, is very different from a disorderly one."

"Yes", said the youth. "From what I have learned from Dionysodorus, in the field of battle, is that we must place the bravest troops in the front and rear, and the cowardly troops in the centre, that they be led on by those in front, and pushed on by those behind."

"Ah", said Socrates, "so he has taught you how to distinguish the brave from the cowardly has he? That distinction may prove useful if he really taught you how to spot that difference in their characters."

"No", said the young man, " he did not tell us how to discern this, so we have to learn that skill for ourselves." "Well, well, you must go back to him and rigorously question him on this point. For if he really knows, and is not quite shameless, he will blush, after taking your money, before sending you away in ignorance."

"Thank you", said the youth. "That is good advice, I will go and test him."

On another occasion, I was with him when he met a person who had recently been elected a General. "Congratulations!" said Socrates, well done! "Now tell me, why is it, do you think, that Homer has styled Agamemnon the 'Shepherd of the People'?"

"I do not know, Socrates", said the newly appointed General.

"Is it not because, just as a shepherd must be watchful that his flock are safe, and have food, so a good General must do the same, so they are fit to conquer the enemy? Similarly why has he praised Agamemnon by saying 'He was both characters, a good king, and an efficient warrior'? "I do not know, Socrates." "Doesn't he mean that he would fail to be an efficient warrior if he had fought alone against the enemy, and had not the skill to inspire courage in his entire army, like a King? And would he not fail to be a good king if he looked after his own subsistence and comfort only and had not looked after the same needs for his people? In short he should render those he commands to be happy and well contented with his Leadership."

The newly appointed General thanked Socrates for his good advice, most profusely, which he valued and would keep well in mind when in the field of battle.

I remember that on another occasion we met a youth who had just been chosen to serve as a Hipparch [cavalry commander - E.R.S.]. "Could you tell me, young man, with what aim in view did you aspire to become a Hipparch? I am sure it was not for the sake of riding first amongst the cavalry, because the horse-archers are always honoured with that place?"

"That is correct", said the youth.

"Well" replied Socrates, "it could not have been merely to be noticed, for even a lunatic can be noticed. Was it that you hoped to make the cavalry more efficient and so prove it to be an advantage to the State? I do hope so, for that would be truly honourable if you could achievet that ambition. For the command you have chosen takes charge of both the horses and their riders."

"It does so, Socrates."

"Well then tell me how you propose to make certain the horses are looked after much better?"

"I do not really consider that is my business. It is up to each man to look after the welfare of his own horse."

"If then some of your men should present you with their horses diseased in their feet, weak in their legs, feeble in their bodies, and so ill-fed, that they could not follow you when you lead them, what would such a cavalry be of use to you or the army?"

"You admonish me well, Socrates. I shall try and see that they look after the horses as far as may be in my power."

"Good, and will you not endeavour to improve your riders?"

"I shall."

"Good. First of all teach them improved ways of mounting their steeds more quickly."

"A good proposal, Socrates. So if any fall off they will be able to get back into the saddle much more quickly."

"Now, when you engage the enemy, will you bring them down to your ground level, or pursue them on the level at which they are placed?"

"In my opinion the latter way would be more effective to assure victory."

"Yes, and will you teach your men the skill of throwing javelins while on horseback?"

"Yes, that will be good too."

"Have you considered how to raise the courage of your men in the face of the enemy?"

"No, Socrates, not yet. But now you have mentioned it, I will do so."

"Have you also considered how your men will be induced to obey you?"

"Not yet, Socrates, please tell me the best way."

"Practice assiduously to be the best horseman amongst them. This will give them confidence in you. Impress upon them by oratory that it is much safer for them to obey your orders than to ignore them."

"Do you mean, I should learn how to make speeches?"

"Yes, of course. You are not going to lead and inspire your troops by silence! Please endeavour to arouse in your men all those exertions which will benefit you as their leader, and their country by their prowess!"

"Yes, I shall, Socrates, thank you for your wise advice. I have learned more this afternoon in a brief meeting than I learned spending many hours with Dionysodorus, who mainly teaches tactics and little else."

"So I have heard, my lad. It is a pity, but we must accept things as they are sometimes, not as we want them. The Gods know best. Farewell."

"Farewell, Socrates, and thank you again!"

[The young, ambitious cavalry officer left, and once again I saw how Socrates assisted our youth for the good of Athens.] I must reemphasise that he was never the corrupting influence, of which he was falsely accused, and led alas, to his death, rather than suffer the disgrace of execution in the eyes of his countrymen.

On another occasion while walking, we met young Pericles the son of the great Pericles. Socrates greeted him and then said, "I have great hopes, Pericles, that under your auspicious leadership our beloved Athens will soon become much more powerful and that you will protect her from her many enemies."

Pericles: I sincerely hope so, dear Socrates, that what you say will happen, but how to achieve this noble aim is my question?

Socrates: I perceive that the City now seems to be more favourably disposed to encourage any good General to succeed. We must remind them all that their forefathers were the most courageous of men. Unfortunately the Athenians after attaining great prowess in military matters, grew neglectful of themselves, and consequently became somewhat degenerate. Yet we must not assume that The Athenians are disordered with an incurable depravity. They are orderly in their naval affairs, gymnastic games, and in their dramatic choruses, if not in other ways.

Pericles: Yet the infantry and cavalry, in my opinion, who should be foremost in valour and virtue are the least well organised of men.

Socrates: Unfortunately most of our Generals take command without the necessary deep study that is necessary for skill in military command. You must recall your father's high principles and put them into practice.

Pericles: If you imply that I have not put sufficient effort into studying his directives, perhaps you are right, and I must do more.

Socrates: If his plans appear satisfactory to you, as they were, endeavour my excellent young friend to act upon them, it will be both an honour to yourself and an advantage to the State.

Pericles: Thank you, Socrates. I am very glad that I met you to receive such good advice which I promise to follow. [Socrates seemed satisfied with the forceful impression he had made on this ambitious young man.]

These are a few of his aphorisms which I took note of from his many conversations and discourses over the years.

Fortitude: I am of the firm opinion, that it is self evident, as with every natural disposition, such as fortitude, that this virtue, can definitely be improved, by rigorous training and assiduous exercise.

Madness: Madness was the opposite of Prudence. For a man to be ignorant of his own true Self was closely bordering on madness. It is a great disorder of the intellectual and spiritual faculty. The unexamined life is not worth living. Know thy Self.

Conduct: The best pursuit for a man or woman is good conduct and righteous behaviour, strongly rooted in virtue.

The Good: Goodness is the noblest virtue that a man or woman is capable of holding. As purified Consciousness, it contains the divine qualities of Love, Truth, Beauty and Wisdom, which are inherent powers implicit in Knowledge of the Self.

Health: It is disgraceful for a man or woman to grow old through self-neglect, before he knows what he would become, by not exercising himself to be well formed and vigorous in mind and body.

Abstinence: Abstain from over indulgence in food and drink. After some abstinence one will live with much more pleasure, far less expense, and considerably better health.

Punishment: Once we saw a man beating his slave most severely. Socrates asked him why he was so angry at his slave. "Because", he said, "he is gluttonous, stupid, covetous and idle." Have you ever reflected" said Socrates "which of the two of you deserves the greater number of stripes, you or your slave?"

Equality: Once at a banquet, some had brought vey little food and others a great quantity. Socrates ordered the attendant to set the smallest dish on the table for common participation and to distribute a portion of it to each. Thus, those who had brought a great deal were shamed into sharing what was put on the table for the company in general. They then offered their own dishes, but received no greater share than those who had brought very little. After this demonstration Socrates said, "Now you will all begin to understand the virtue of Equality. We must be equal and moderate in all things never giving way to extremes of thought or feeling in mind or body. The secret of temperance is not to take anything in excess."

Education: A man is a stupid arrogant fool who believes he can distinguish between the good and evil in life without right education from one who has conquered the passions and is detached in his dealings with the world, and is rich in Self Knowledge. Worldly wealth cannot buy Virtue or Self Knowledge. Dependence on natural abilities or acquired wealth alone, without right education ftomm an Awakened Master, is vain and would lead to an impoverished spirit.

Self Knowledge: Once I was with Socrates when we met a

young, intelligent member of his circle named Euthydemus. The memorable conversation after the usual greetings went like this...."

Socrates: Tell me Euthydemus, have you ever been to Delphi?

Euthedymus: Yes twice, Socrates.

Socrates: Did you observe what was inscribed on the temple wall?

Euthedymus: I certainly did, Socrates, the injunction to Know Thy Self.

Socrates: Well, then, did you attend to it, and seriously make the effort to enquire into your Self, and see the True Nature that you have?

Euthedymus: No. Socrates, I thought I knew, my characteristics already,.

Socrates: Do you really think that Self Examination is like people buying a horse, just to know whether it is fit for riding and the chase? It is much more than merely knowing your bodily, mental and emotional characteristics. That is child's play. Self Knowledge is a much greater acquisition than that. It is the most important act that a man or woman can ever undertake if they really wish to awaken from the dream of life, which merely means they are living in the play of the senses, rather than obtaining the blissful Wisdom in the Absolute Goodness of their purified Awareness which is their Divine Self. That is true happiness, not wealth, riches, family, sexual pleasures, entertainment, athletic prowess, and all the foolish diversions that men and women ignorantly think will make them truly contented. These are passing, transient, enjoyments which inevitably carry pain and suffering in their wake.

Euthedymus: I never really considered it to mean an endeavour so important as that, Socrates. Tell me how I may acquire such wisdom?

Socrates: Hard application, perseverance, effort, faith and determination, dear boy. Pray to the Gods to enlighten you.

Yearn to Know Thy Self through turning your mind inwards and looking for the source of your false sense of 'me' which is a fiction, not the Real I Am, which is your own true Self. Surrender to the will of the Good, which is inside your heart, abandon all worry and anxiety. Everything will gradually unfold. Trust the great power of your own Self which knows the way! Contemplate and meditate on that.

Euthydemus: [somewhat overawed] Thank you so much, dear Socrates. You are truly a Great Master. I will try and practice what you say.

Socrates: Very good, my lad. Come and visit me whenever you want, especially when you meet difficulties. Let me know how you get on. Now Aeschines, we must move on. Give him one of your superb sausages, the baby rabbit and lamb, with honey, black pepper and thyme are far the best, in my opinion.

[I could continue with many anecdotes concerning my great master, but, as I do not wish to weary the reader, I shall close with my memory of him in prison.]

Chapter 8

Socrates in Prison

This is the account of the time I spent with Socrates when I visited him in prison after he was falsely accused by Miletus for corrupting the youth of Rome. This was a dreadful calumny. Such was the jealousy of certain factions in Athens at the time that charges were trumped up against him, and corrupt Judges found him guilty on hearsay evidence which consisted of lies. I urged Socrates to escape and offered to assist him, but he refused to accept any ignominy and preferred an honourable death. Plato attributed this offer of escape to his friend Crito because he was jealous of my close friendship with the Master. But it was I, not Crito who offered him help to gain his freedom.

I said to Socrates:

"Listen well Socrates, I implore you with all my heart. It would not take very much money to bribe certain people to set you free and get you out of the country. I will offer all the money that I have, so will Simias of Thebes, and Kebes is ready too. I suggest Thessaly, as a refuge where I have many friends who would only be too pleased to look after you. No one there could ever touch you. We feel it is wrong of you to sacrifice yourself deliberately, when you could be saved. If we delay any longer, it may not be possible. Listen to me Socrates, I beg you, please do not say No!"

Socrates: We should never, ever do anything which might be judged or appear to be wrong in they eyes of our fellows willingly. That is the first and most important principle. Let us leave it the way it is, dear Aeschines. This is the way that God has preordained it. I would rather surrender to His almighty will, and have an honourable death at my own hand, and become one with my maker in perfect peace for Eternity, then live a life as a refugee from Justice, as the State decreed, and then having commited the heinious sin of bribery. Let us now leave it alone, my dear Aeschines, go Sausage Maker, I thank you for your love and loyal friendship. If you wish to serve me well, then write a record of my Discourses and Dialogues from the notes you have carefully taken. This will be a greater service to me, then I fear will be left by that young ambitious Plato, keen to further his own reputation as a Philosopher. You will enlighten future generations. This is much better than risking a hazardous escape which defies the Gods and consequently will certainly lead to disaster. Say no more Aeschines. Go now. [he spoke with such great emphasis and authority, that it was impossible for me to disobey him] Socrates warmly embraced me, and with tears in my eyes I left him. This is my final record of this great man, who always unfailingly pointed us to the Truth, which now I leave for the education and betterment of future generations.

So ends the records, I discovered in Cairo, by the very best of good fortune, a few of those lost dialogues of Aeschines. I have translated them faithfully to the very best of my ability. In the event of my death I have arranged for them to be published posthumously, Dr. Ernest R. Sekers.

BOOKS